BOOK ONE OF THE EVERLASTING TRILOGY

DIAMONDS NICOLE WATSON

ISBN: 978-1-60414-703-2

Book Cover Design by Navid Mehedi

Story consultant: Robin Surface

This book is a work of fiction. Names, characters, places, incidents are either the product of the author's imagination or are used fictitiously. Any resemblance to actual persons, living or dead, events, or locales is entirely coincidental.

Dedications

First and foremost, I want to Thank God for this gift, this journey of self-discovery my writing has took me on, and everything that has followed. To my daughter, thank you for always believing in me. For always having pride in what I do whether you understand why I do it, or not.

Thank you to Erica, Kelvin, Eli, my family, and my Spirit Sisters. You all are an exceptional group of people. Thank you for walking in your own truth, conquering the darkness with such grace, and inspiring me to do the same. Enjoy!

Chapter 1

A little over two months ago, I faced my fears, left my ex and started over.

I met the toxic waste cloud, otherwise known as Ashton Reynolds, when I was a sophomore at Georgia State University. We had an econ class together and had our professor not been fired, we might not have met. Our replacement professor decided our final needed to be some bullshit teamwork thing that had us working in groups of four. Ashton and I got stuck with a couple of dim bulbs and ended up doing all the work.

We spent a lot of time together, and you know that old cliché about familiarity leading to attraction... in our case, it was true.

I've always had issues with people. The problem wasn't that I couldn't make friends, it was that I always seemed to attract the wrong type of friends. You know, the ones who were only friendly because they needed something from me. I'd help them pass a class, spend my time studying with them and thinking we were friends. Then once the test was over or they passed the class, they'd ghost me. It happened so often that I just quit trying to find a "real" friend.

1

Ash, as he asked me to call him not long after we started working together, was a breath of fresh air. He wasn't threatened by my brains because we were intellectual equals. Once we took our study relationship to the next level, I would fall asleep in his arms almost every night. I thought I'd finally found someone who understood me.

We were inseparable for the next two years. The problem was we never talked about what was going to happen after graduation. I was under the impression that our futures were connected, but then I found out he hadn't really thought about *our* future at all. That should have been a red flag. Most girls on campus who had been with their guys that long were running around showing off the huge rock on their fingers. I sometimes worried that Ash would never propose and would eventually leave me, but I brushed this off as leftover feelings of abandonment from my childhood.

When graduation time was upon us, I put on a brave face and waited to see what my future was going to be. Ash had been applying for jobs for months, and I was left waiting to find a job myself because I wanted him to find his place first so that I could guarantee I'd be at his side.

Ash and I both graduated *cum laude,* and I thought we were finally going to start our lives together. The thought at the back of my mind all along was that he was waiting to pop the question until we got through the stress of finishing school and graduation. Damn, I was naïve.

Chapter 2

Two weeks after graduation, Ash flew to Seattle for an interview with Pendleton & Wilkins, a fancy PR firm that worked with big name celebrities. He came back with a job and suggested that I come along with him to Seattle. Of course, I said yes.

We only had two weeks to get our living situation figured out before he started work. So, we found something quickly and signed a lease.

Our time in Seattle started out pretty well. We settled in, learned the area, and explored. The only down side to this was that I had to find a job near our new home. I convinced myself that something would present itself, but I was wrong.

Time went so quickly, and before I knew it months had gone by and I still hadn't found a job in my field. I refused to settle for something less than what I wanted. At first, Ash understood. He couldn't imagine having to accept some bullshit position, so I thought he didn't want that for me either.

When the six month mark came and went and I still hadn't found anything, he became more impatient with me. He started calling me selfish because he was the only one bringing in a paycheck. My thinking was, I'd dedicated all that time and money to getting my degree and I just wasn't ready to give up finding a job where I could use it.

After several more months went by with no great job offers, I finally realized Seattle wasn't a great place for me career-wise. Not one to give up easily, I decided to try a different a route and get my doctorate. I wanted to learn the logistics of finance, economics, and marketing. In my mind, going back to school was definitely better than being unemployed.

I told Ash about my plans, and he was all for it ... until he wasn't. After a while, he began complaining constantly about having to pay for everything with no help from me. He resented me and I could see things were going to get worse if I didn't do something soon. So, I began splitting all the bills with him, even though I had to spend some of my inheritance to do it.

I was enrolled at Rowan and was surprised by how much I loved it. I was making real friends there and thriving. I didn't feel alienated, and no one used my brains against me there. I had an amazing day, every day — at least until I got home.

Ash and I were quickly moving toward living separate lives. We had different goals, friends, and experiences. It was like we barely knew each other. We'd lost our connection.

I was almost positive Ash was sleeping with someone else, but I chose to ignore it. I didn't want to go through the hassle of moving and face being alone again, so instead I just looked the other way and remained cocooned in my comfortable bubble.

I was in survival mode. I just had to hold on until I could finish my doctorate and join the workforce. I was sure things would go back to normal after I was bringing in a paycheck. That's what I told myself, anyway. So, that's exactly what I did until I completed my PhD.

I had everything planned, and was sure I was reading the situation correctly. Again, I had things completely wrong. I was in denial, plain and simple.

Instead of celebrating after my graduation ceremony, Ash dropped me off at the apartment and left me there by myself. So, on what was supposed to be one of the best days of my life — the day I fulfilled my promise to Gram — I was alone, crying myself to sleep.

My life after that was nothing like what my friends were experiencing. There was no traveling, exploring, or living my best life — I was frantically job hunting so I could get my life back on track. I applied to every job I found, and soon realized my new degree wasn't as much help as I'd hoped. My prospects were bleak and I was quickly descending into depression.

One day, Ash came home grinning from ear to ear. I was confused by this, because I rarely saw him happy anymore. Ash's excitement created an unexpected light in my otherwise dark day, and I was happy to have my best friend back, even if it was just for the moment.

Ash told me Gina, his personal assistant, had resigned with no notice.

"That's too bad. Why did she resign?" I asked as I watched his smile disappear like it had never been there.

"Who the fuck cares *why*? The fact is she *did!* Don't you get it? You can take her position. Do you want it or not?"

I'm over-qualified to be his assistant, but I have to start somewhere. Right? I rationalized. My self-confidence was at an all-time low, so I smiled like it was the best news I'd ever heard. "That's a great idea, Ash. I'll apply right away.

I began working for Ash at the firm the following Monday morning. It wasn't quite what I expected. It was a glamorous job, even for a lowly assistant. There were fancy parties and premieres, plus I was on a first name basis with several big Hollywood celebrities. Several of them even tried to lure me away with job offers, which was a great self-confidence builder for me. Being wanted by people like that was an amazing feeling.

While this type of attention didn't increase the size of my ego, the same couldn't be said for Ash. I watched from the sidelines as he turned into someone unrecognizable. Suddenly, I wasn't good enough for him, our perfect little apartment was beneath him, and he was under the impression that he was someone too special to interact with the "little" people in his life.

As we ate breakfast in silence one morning, Ash asked if I could sit in on a meeting with Alexander Malone the following day. Alexander, who was one of my favorite actors, had been working as a celebrity guest host for *ET*, and the firm was renegotiating his contract because the network had asked him to stay on. The short notice for the meeting was because this was the only day that Malone could fit a meeting into his busy schedule. I'd met him a few times, and he always seemed down to earth and genuine, not to mention he was absolutely gorgeous — not that I was interested ... much.

The following day, I managed to make it to the office an hour before the meeting was scheduled to start. Ash was gone when I got up, so I expected him to be there when I arrived. His car wasn't in the lot and another car was parked in his space. As I walked by, a very agitated Alexander Malone got out of that car and blocked my path.

After introducing myself, I invited him to come inside with me and we talked about the weather and his flight as we waited for Ash to make an appearance. Malone was intelligent, and surprisingly humble, which was a refreshing change compared to some of the celebrities I'd been dealing with.

Eventually, he calmed down a bit and told me that he'd tried to reach Ash to let him know he would be early, but got no response. Since today was the only day he was free, he said he took a chance that someone would be here and just showed up.

We ended up talking for nearly 45 minutes before Ash finally came strolling through the door. He took one look at our chummy conversation and gave me a glare of pure resentment. It was at that moment I realized this man was nothing like the person I'd fallen in love with. I had the sinking suspicion our relationship really was over and had been for a long time, and I suddenly felt completely alone.

Regardless of how I felt after this epiphany, I was at work and needed to stay professional. I could fall apart later, when I didn't have an audience.

They went into Ash's office, and I stayed at my desk. An hour later, Alex, as he'd asked me to call him, came out and made his way to my desk.

"Is everything okay?" I asked, confused by the frown on his face.

"Sure," he said, stopping a foot from my desk.

"How did the meeting go?" I asked, trying to determine what I'd missed.

"It went like all of my meetings with Ash, unfortunately. That's why I've decided to hire another firm."

"I apologize about today, it was my—"

"Please don't make excuses for him. I get the feeling you have to do that a lot. Don't waste your breath. He's a pompous ass, and I don't have to put up with that. ... Ms. Walker, may I speak frankly?"

"Sure."

"The only way I will remain with this firm is if you handle my account."

Shock was my first reaction, then came fear. Not that I couldn't do it, but that this would be the final nail in the coffin for me and Ash.

"Mr. Malone, while I appreciate the thought, I'm not an agent. I'm just a PA, so I'm not qualified. You're better off with Mr. Reynolds."

Alex didn't say anything at first, just studied the photo on my desk. "I saw a picture of you in cap and gown on Ash's desk. In this one you're wearing a different cap and gown."

"Different graduations from different schools. I've got a BA in business administration and a PhD in public relations."

"Wow. Congratulations. Why are you working as a PA? Couldn't you find a job where you could use your degree, or did Ash decide you should do *this* job so he could keep you under his thumb?"

"Excuse me?" I ask, stunned by his question.

"I mean, I can think of several major agencies who are looking for agents. You would be a great agent. You have good people skills and you seem dedicated. So, why stay here when you're so overqualified for this job? If it's for him, I can tell you right now he's not worth it. In fact, from what I've seen, he's not worthy of you. Don't think I didn't notice the way he treats you. So, *why* you are here?"

I didn't say anything, because I didn't want to admit it to myself. Deep down, I knew — I stayed out of fear. Fear that I wouldn't find a place to live, fear that I wouldn't find someone to be with... Suddenly I felt Alex's warm, strong hands clasping mine.

"Look, I figured you had some kind of relationship with him, and the lost look in your eyes just proved it. You're an intelligent woman. You have to know he'll never respect you if you continue to be his PA. You won't respect yourself, either. I'm going to give you a chance to be more."

"What do you mean?"

"People fascinate me. I like to study them so much that I made a career out of it. After speaking with you for just a short time, I feel like you're someone I want on my team. It's your decision. Either become my new agent or the firm will lose my business."

I sat there staring at him, stunned into silence. What he was offering me was an amazing opportunity. But, if I took it things would change drastically in my life.

"I'll give you a week to decide. Here's my card — my personal cell is written on the back. Call me when you make the right decision."

When I got home that evening, I made dinner and waited for Ash. He finally walked through the door two hours later.

"Are you hungry?"

"Well, last I checked, I'm human and I just home from work. You tell me."

I made a plate for him, and waited until he was nice and settled before making my move. I'd fortified myself with a bit of liquid courage in the form of wine so I wouldn't lose my nerve. "Are there any openings at the firm for a new agent?"

"Do I look like fucking HR?" he asked, rolling his eyes.

"No, but you usually know what's going on there."

"Well, that's not something I'd know."

"*Really?* Well, I happen to know there's an opening and I've applied for it."

He looked up from his plate, his eyes as hard as steel. This time, I gave him the look right back. "I spoke to Mr. Malone after your meeting today. He's ready to take his business elsewhere unless I take over as his agent. He made it clear he would *not* be staying if he had to continue working with you.

"Want to know why Ash?" I asked, rushing to say my piece before he had a chance to start yelling. "It seems he thinks you can't be bothered to show up on time or be polite or even act remotely professional when dealing with your clients. He told me he doesn't think you're interested in representing him, you just want his money.

"The sad thing is, he's not alone in thinking this way. Several of your other clients have expressed the same dissatisfaction. I'm the one who ends up smoothing things out with them so they'll keep working with you. You deserve to lose the Malone account, and the others too. I'm actually more qualified than you, so I'm going to be the best damn agent the firm has ever seen."

"I pull strings to get you a job because you couldn't find one on your own, and *this* is how you repay me?"

"Strings, huh? I spoke with the firm's president today. When I told him I was interested in applying for the open position, he was genuinely surprised. He had no idea that I was qualified. He told me that position had been open for a long time — since before I graduated. Why didn't you tell me about it? ... Let me guess, you didn't want to have to compete with me so you decided I should be your PA. Yeah, that's really pulling some strings there, Ash.

"After I told the president about Mr. Malone's ultimatum, he agreed that transferring the account to me was better than losing it. So, I got a promotion today."

"You know what? Do what you want, but don't expect me to be your cheerleader. He's all yours," Ash said, barely containing his anger. "I'm leaving. I'd rather sleep under a bridge with rats crawling up my ass than be here with you." And then he was gone. For the first time, I welcomed his absence.

The following day, I walked into the office to a huge surprise. One of the rooms we used to store office supplies had been turned into my new office. I was ecstatic, even though it was a smaller office than Ash's. Everyone was happy for me, well except for Ash. My first call from my new office was to Mr. Malone so I could let him know that I was officially his new agent. As soon as we finished the call, I emailed over the necessary paperwork for him to sign. Once that was done, I had my first client!

***

Alex and I became fast friends, and he filled nearly all the holes left open by Ash's lack of interest — best friend, therapist, savior, coach, cheerleader, etc. The only thing missing was romance. Sometimes, I would sense an attraction on his part, but Alex respected the fact that I wasn't ready to begin a new romance — plus I was still living with Ash.

I'd been trying to come to terms with the end of my relationship. My attempts at hoping, wishing, crying, and praying that we could work it out had finally dried up. For some reason though, I just couldn't quite let go of my romanticized version of my relationship with Ash. I often wondered if what we had was really love. I'd think of the good times through the years, and I'd convince myself it was real and maybe it could be real again. So, I kept waiting for him to come to his senses and sweep me off my feet so I wouldn't have to be my own again.

Chapter 3

My hope for a happily ever after kind of ending for Ash and me soon died a swift death. At 4:30 a.m., I strolled into my office, feeling refreshed from a fun weekend. Alex had taken me with him to a celebrity event in Puerto Rico and paid for my suite at an all-inclusive resort because he said I needed a vacation. The weekend was amazing and I was so grateful to him. The pampering and me-time was just what I needed.

I was relaxed, happy and smiling when I stepped off the elevator. I made my way to my office, turned on the lights and sat down at my desk. I opened my desk drawer and the draft of the renewed contract Alex had approved with VH1 and ET was gone.

I checked the other desk drawers, but the contracts weren't there. I knew I put them there before I left for the weekend. Starting to panic, I searched the entire office, but still couldn't find them. *Maybe I gave them to my assistant and just forgot?*

I grabbed my cell and called her.

"Hello?" a sleepy voice answered.

"Hey, Adrienne, it's Lena. I'm sorry to call so early, but it's important. Do you have the drafts of Mr. Malone's revised contracts in your desk?"

"No, I thought you had them."

Shit! "No, I don't. I'll keep looking. I'll see you in a few hours. Sorry for waking you."

I tried to calm down and retrace my steps. *There has to be an explanation. Maybe I—*

Crash!

What the hell was that? That sounded like glass hitting the floor and breaking, but as far as I know I'm the only one here. Is someone robbing the place? I grabbed a paperweight, which was the only thing handy that resembled a weapon, and put my phone in my pocket, then slipped my heels off in case I had to run.

I stepped out of my office, bending low so no one could see me, and looked around. All the cubicles and offices were dark, except for one. As I get closer to that office, I heard more noises. *If someone's robbing the place, they're either crazy or really bad at this, because they sure as hell aren't being stealthy.*

I realized the light was coming from Ash's office. *I should let his ass get robbed,* I thought. But, of course, I couldn't really let that happen. I grabbed my phone, prepared to dial 911, and quietly slipped into the small space near the door where I could see through the crack.

When my brain registered what my eyes were seeing, my phone and the paperweight slid right out of my hands. I couldn't move or speak, all I could do was watch with horrified fascination.

Ash was standing at his desk, naked as the day he was born, with his pants pooled at his feet, and a pair of Manolo Blahniks hooked on either side of his hips. *He's fucking some tramp on his desk! Seriously?* All I could hear was the slapping of flesh, and Ash's breathing. His thrusts are so powerful that his desk drawers are rattling. I look down and saw glass all over the floor, which explained the noise I heard.

Just then the woman started yelling, "Ahh, yes, Ash! Yes, baby! Fuck me harder! Fuck this pussy, baby. Yes! Just like that!"

Not to be outdone by his whore, Ash shouted, "That's right, baby. Take my big dick! Take it all!" He seemed to be excited by his own words, and pumped harder and faster, hooking his hands around her legs so he could pull her forward to meet his thrusts. *God, this is like watching a bad porno,* I thought, as I stood there mesmerized.

"Ooh, shit, baby. I'm gonna cum!"

"Cum for me, baby! I want you to paint this dick with that pretty pussy juice!"

"Oh, shit! Ohhh… Ahhh! She screamed even louder, apparently finding her release. *She's got to be faking. No woman actually says that when she's cuming. Does she?*

I'm was transfixed by what I was witnessing, so I kept watching as Ash fell forward, laying his head on her breasts, panting.

He finally decided to stand up, but the woman wasn't having it. "What do you think you're doing? You're not done."

"I'm not?" he asked as he took two fingers and slowly played with her wet pussy.

"Ah, yes, baby. Keep doing that."

He looked right at her and started to lick his wet fingers. "Nope."

"What the fuck do you mean no? I'm not done!"

"Exactly what I said. I'm the boss of you and you're gonna sit that sexy pussy on my face."

As she got up, I could finally see her face. *Gina, Ash's former assistant! What the fuck?*

I keep watching as he took her place on the desk and she climbed on top of him and spread her thighs on either side of his head, then she lowered her pussy directly onto his mouth. She started to slowly grind on his tongue, and then bent and sucked his dick into her mouth.

"Ah, yes! Suck it good, bitch!" he shouted into her pussy, as he held her ass in his hands. After that, he went back to eating her pussy like a starving man at a buffet.

I'm having an out of body experience. That was the only explanation my overloaded brain can find as I watch my man fuck another woman. Even now, with the evidence right in front of me, my poor brain couldn't comprehend what this meant. *Ash never wanted to 69 with me*, I thought, feeling betrayed and hurt.

What was worse, my body was reacting in an inappropriate way to this x-rated show — I was turned on. I felt like I was about to explode. I'd never felt this way about Ash before, so I closed my eyes and thought of the one guy who could make me cum, as I slipped my hand under my skirt.

My hand made its way inside my panties and I stroked my pussy. *Damn, I'm wet.* I kept watching the Ash and Gina Show as Gina ground her pussy on Ash's face. *He's so deep into her that I can only see the back of his head*, I marveled.

"Don't stop! I'm cuming! I'm gonna cum. Don't you dare stop!" she screamed, then started deep-throating his dick.

She stopped again and yelled, "Eat me harder, baby. Yesss! Oh, God!" She came so hard she was shaking and rubbing her pussy over his face. When she stilled, Ash gave her ass two taps, and she climbed off him.

He stood up and pointed to the floor. "On your knees. Now! Make me cum."

She dropped to her knees, took his dick in her hands, and started stroking. She licked the tip, circling her tongue a few times before she deep throated it again. Ash grabbed a handful of her hair and pulled it, tipping her head back so he could fuck the shit out of her mouth, and she took it.

"Deeper! Yeah! That's it! Now, I want those titties. Give them to me," he demanded as he pulled out of her mouth. She sat up on her knees and grabbed her breasts, pushing them together. He started fucking her between them as she pushed them together. Then, she bent her head down and sucked his tip in with each thrust.

"I'm cuming!" he yelled as he pumped faster and faster.

As I watched, I was finger-fucking my pussy with one hand and pinching my nipple with the other, matching their rhythm. I pinched my nipple hard, and experienced a feeling of euphoria as I came on my fingers. When I'd recovered, I bend down, grabbed my paperweight and phone and got ready to sneak back to my office.

"So, do you need me to dispose of the contracts on my way out?" Gina asked, as she licked the cum from her lips.

Dispose of the contracts? My contracts? That has to be what she's talking about. The bitch doesn't even work here anymore! I looked back through the crack in the door, and watched as they both put their clothes on.

"I don't know. I didn't think past seeing them on her desk and taking them. I can't believe she got them to re-sign Malone. I was sure he was on his way out. How the hell did she do it?"

"I know, I was there. Remember?" Gina said.

"Oh, yeah. I remember you being there. I remember *every-thing* I ever got from you, starting with my first week here. You gave me quite the welcome, baby."

"Well, I aim to please."

It was time for me to go, in more ways than one, and I knew just what I was going to do. After witnessing that scene, I realized it truly was over between Ash and me. After the initial shock, I felt no real no emotions at all about what they were doing, other than feeling horny. It really was like watching a porno starring strangers, not my cheating boyfriend.

Later that day, after I finished packing all of my things, I took a little detour to Ash's office. When I walked in, he was sitting in his chair reading the paper.

"Well, hello," I said.

"What the fuck do you want?"

"I was taking one last stroll around this place. I just turned in my resignation," I said calmly.

"Malone dropped your ass too, huh? Well, I guess karma really is a bitch," he said, and couldn't hide his pure glee at the thought of something bad happening to me.

I took a seat in front of his desk, and got comfortable. "I'm sorry to disappoint you, but he didn't drop me. Mr. Malone and several of your other clients have learned that good help is hard to find, so they'll be finding other representation too. By the way, what did you decide to do with them?" I asked, relishing his bewildered expression.

"Do with what?"

He looks genuinely lost, bless his heart. "Malone's contracts, of course. I know you took them. Actually, I know a lot of things now. It's amazing what you can learn when you come to work early. Of course, if you'd paid any attention to me since I started this job, you'd know I often come in early to get a jump on the day. Unlike you, who apparently comes in early to get a jump on your slutty former assistant. Great show, by the way."

He didn't comment, only looked at me. I took that as my cue to continue. "So, after my *informative* morning, I had a little chat with the bosses. I told them I suspected you'd taken the contracts from my desk, and they ran the security footage to find out for sure. I was making a pretty serious accusation, after all. Of course, you taking the contracts off my desk wasn't the only thing they saw," I said, smiling and looking him directly in the eyes.

"Nothing to say? That's okay. I understand. I've got plenty to say, so you can just listen. They told me my suspicions were confirmed, and I'm positive they'll be saying more than that to you, since they also had to see you fucking your former assistant on top of your desk. I'm sure they had a great view too, since there's a camera in your office. Crazy, huh? So, maybe you should take your last stroll too. I have no doubt that right this minute they're discussing how and when to fire you."

The look on Ash's face was priceless. *The firm's golden boy suddenly realizes he has a lead parachute! Poor baby.*

"Well, I have to go. Things to do, people to see and all that," I said as I walked to the door, then turned to make my parting shot, "Oh, and just so you know, you never could fuck worth a damn. I'm pretty sure Gina was faking it this morning — probably every time you've fucked her too. I doubt she'll stick around now that you don't have access to all those celebrity clients. ... See ya, wouldn't want to be ya."

As I walked away, I wanted to laugh and cry at the same time. I'd wasted all that time trying to make things work with that asshole because I refused to see him for what he was, and that was tearing me up. But, knowing he was going to get exactly what he deserved put a little smile on my face, and I walked with confidence as I gathered my things from my office and left to start the next part of my life.

When I got to my car, I called Alex and told him everything, excluding my little voyeuristic pleasure session. He asked me to consider moving in with him until I could find my own place, but I had to turn him down. I needed some time by myself so I could face my fear of being alone. When we finished our call, I booked a hotel.

After a few days of self-contemplation, I decided staying in Seattle wasn't in the cards for me. I told Alex I was going back home to Atlanta, and he understood. I lined up another excellent agent for Alex and the rest of Ash's former clients, since I didn't want to leave them hanging. Alex, wasn't happy about this turn of events, but eventually understood. He even insisted I stay at his home until I could get things ready in Atlanta.

I finally gave in and took him up on his offer. I wouldn't see him much while I was there because he was working long hours. I was glad about that, since he wasn't exactly thrilled about me moving to Atlanta and kept trying to change my mind every chance he got.

I was going to live in Gram's house, so I had lots of things to plan and put into motion before my move. I hired a company to retrieve all of my things from Ash's apartment and put them in storage. They would be delivered to Atlanta once I'd made the move.

Next, with Alex's help, I found a contractor to check out the house and tell me what needed to be done to make it livable, since it had been standing empty for so long. The contractor had good news for me, and I'd be moving home in a couple of months.

***

Two months later, I was waving goodbye to Alex as I boarded a plane for Atlanta. I promised him we'd get together as soon as I got settled.

But, settling in took longer than I expected, and in the last three months I've hardly even spoken to poor Alex. Our schedules were hectic, which made staying in touch difficult and planning a visit nearly impossible.

Chapter 4

The move back to Atlanta turned out to be a good thing almost immediately. The timing was perfect and I landed the president's position at the Good Samaritan's Foundation. There were some extenuating circumstances involved with how the position came to be open, but I really didn't care.

Three months into the job, I was summoned to an unscheduled meeting with the board. I was terrified they were going to fire me. Instead, I was pleasantly surprised because they said they were impressed by what I'd accomplished in such a short time and wanted me to mastermind a project that would help to repair the Foundation's reputation.

To make their plan work, I had to gain the cooperation of an extremely private celebrity who wasn't known for his altruistic side. The board wanted me to get him on-board so we didn't lose our biggest investors, whose confidence had been shaken by the former president's illegal activities.

They told me I had six months to make this happen. If I couldn't get him to agree to work with us in some way by then, the Foundation's future would be on shaky ground.

I guess my skepticism was written all over my face because Susan McKinley, my boss and president of the board said, "Lena, we know this is a lot to ask when you've been here for such a short time, but we have faith in you. You've worked miracles for us already — you've basically saved this organization through your amazing PR efforts after the whole embezzlement scandal hit the news. Now, we need you to save it again, but in a different way.

"You didn't get this job because you're just another pretty face. The Foundation chose you because we saw your potential. You're the right leader for us, and with the right leader, anything is possible. That said, let's get you briefed on your target."

Two hours later, I walked out of the room feeling like I'd been hit by a truck. This was going to be a challenge, but the kids that would receive the Foundation's help were more than deserving. The deadline wasn't really a problem — I thrive under pressure. The problem was my "target" as Susan had dubbed him. It was none other than Jonah Parker, or JJ as I'd known him in another life — my first love.

So, my prized president's position was suddenly hanging in the balance and all I had to do to save it was land an exclusive contract with a ghost from my past. *How fucking cruel can God be?*

Alex was my first thought after I got my new "assignment." I crossed my fingers that he'd have time to talk, and called him the first chance I got. Luck was with me and we got to talk for a long time. I eventually told him about the nearly impossible task I'd been given, and asked if he could pull any strings for me or at least point me in the right direction so I could complete it. He said he'd try, but it might take some time.

Three weeks later, I'd used every contact I had, as well as trying some not-so-nice tactics, and I still hadn't spoken to the elusive Jonah Parker. I realized the board hadn't been exaggerating when they said he was difficult to reach. So, I decided to try something different.

In business, as in life, it's all about who you know. Lucky for me I knew someone who never missed his mark and he just also happened to be my best friend. Alex had connections in the entertainment industry, and I was going to push him hard for his help with this. Once I'd mentioned it to him, Alex had said he might be able to point me in the right direction, which was Alex-speak for he'd have to talk to the man himself before he could tell me anything. I was positive that he and Jonah Parker were friends, so it was time to apply some added friendly pressure.

Alex said he didn't have Jonah's phone number, which I didn't really believe, but he did give me the next best thing — his address. Alex had conditions before he'd given me the info though. He made me promise to never reveal where I got the address, and I had to accompany him to an event of his choosing. I agreed in a heartbeat. Everything was falling into place.

I decided to send a candid and slightly coercive letter to try to convince the elusive Jonah "JJ" Parker to cooperate with me.

> *Mr. Parker,*
>
> *I would like to speak to you about a potential partnership with the Good Samaritan's Foundation. I know that you have declined to meet with us in the past, but I hope to change your mind.*
>
> *I am aware of your medical history and the time you spent on the UNOS list awaiting a heart donor. The people and families all over the country that benefit from our Foundation's existence are like you once were ... held in suspended ani-*

mation while waiting for donors. Will you be the one who stands in the way of them receiving the life-saving help they need?

The Foundation has drawn up a business proposal that benefits both parties and we think ours would be a great partnership.

I know this is not the conventional way to ask for a meeting, but I have exhausted every other avenue and been turned away by your people. I must warn you, I am dedicated to my job and I will not accept no for an answer.

Can you really dismiss this offer and all of the potential good we could do by working together? At least hear our proposal before deciding.

The Foundation is giving you an opportunity to change people's lives for the better. You, of all people, know how that feels.

Please give me a call or email me so that we can set up a meeting.

Sincerely,
L. Walker, president
The Good Samaritans Foundation
770-555-1212
l.walker.@tgsf.com

Well, I hope that does it. Surely, he can't turn me down, I thought with more confidence than I actually had. I've practically told him he's a villain if he doesn't help.

***

Chapter 5

"**M**s. *Walker, you have a call on line one,*" Veronica, my passive-aggressive personal assistant called out in her syrupy-sweet voice over the intercom, startling me from my thoughts. She was annoying and not really very good at her job, but for some reason I hadn't fired her yet.

She's never liked me, probably because I replaced her embezzling friend Crystal as president of the Foundation. It's not my fault her friend was a criminal and all-around terrible person who prevented sick people from getting the funding they needed. Still, it irritated me that she thought I was the bad guy.

Not many people have this number, so I'd better put on my game face, I thought before picking up the call. "Lena Walker speaking. How may I help you?"

"Is this the *president?*" the voice on the other end asked sarcastically.

Great, someone who thinks he's funny. "Yes, sir. How may I help you?"

"After everything you went through to get me to reach out to you, I think *you* need to tell me."

"I'm sorry. To whom am I speaking?"

"I didn't say. … So, *Ms. President,* do you stalk, emotionally blackmail and generally harass all of your potential donors or am I special?"

A shiver went down my spine and I couldn't find my voice.

"Nothing to say? Haven't you figured out who this is yet?

It can't be, I thought, starting to panic. "Mr. Parker?" I finally choked out.

"Ding-ding-ding! You figured it out. I have to admit, it's kind of fun to torture the woman who's seems to like to play mind games with me. If your behavior is indicative of how your organization is run, then I can see exactly why your group is barely credible."

Shit, shit, shit! I should've known this was coming. I just didn't think it would be so damn soon. I desperately tried to think of something to say to gain control of the situation, but before I could say anything, he was talking again.

"Why don't you just give me a call when you figure out how to speak. In the meantime, you have one chance to pitch your proposal — this seven o'clock this evening at the restaurant in the downtown Westin. I'll tell you now, your prospects aren't good, especially if you never speak. Have a good day *Ms. President.*"

The line went dead. *Fuck, he hung up on me!* For the first time since I've been in this position, I feel incompetent. After running through the conversation in my head for five minutes straight, I still don't know how to feel.

I can't believe JJ just called me. Well, technically he called the "president," but that's me. Granted, he just handed me my ass on a silver platter, but he wants to meet.

On the other hand, he obviously dislikes the way I've been hounding him to get him to meet with me. This is not the scenario I had in mind, but beggars can't be choosers.

Chapter 6

J ust hearing JJ's voice again brought back a flood of memories. The crazy thing was, I was no stranger to writing letters to him. I used to write letters to him about everything I
was doing. But that was a lifetime ago, and I can't help thinking
about it now that he's suddenly back in my life.

Our first encounter was nearly 15 years ago. He wasn't going
by Jonah back then, to me, he was just plain JJ. We met in the
hospital the day I learned that Gram would soon be leaving this
world.

I'd been sitting in her room, next to her bed, holding her
hand and saying every prayer known to man. I begged God to
let her get up and walk out of the hospital so we could both go
home. I denied she was dying, and didn't want to face the fact
that I would soon be alone in the world.

This wasn't the way things were supposed to happen. We still
had places to go and things to see. I also had more to learn from
her. I wasn't ready to let her go.

Selena, my egg donor, was speaking with the doctor in the
hall, trying to discreetly discuss Gram's condition, but I could
hear everything.

"Ms. Walker, I have some very difficult news," the doctor said. "I'm sorry to report that there's been no improvement. Our latest tests show the cancer has spread from her lungs to her other organs. I'm sorry, but there's nothing more we can do for her. It's just a matter of time now."

Hearing those words, I squeezed Gram's hand, pleading with God for a miracle. *What will I do without her? Where will I go? She's the only one who's ever loved me.*

Selena had made it clear over the years that she had no interest in me. Gazing at Gram's frail body with the IVs and tubes sticking out of it, I felt sick to my stomach. It was suddenly too much to bear, so I ran out of the room, ignoring the doctor and Selena as I ran past.

Gram was my best friend — my everything — and knowing I'd be losing her soon was devastating. So, I walked the halls, with my feet moving of their own accord, trying desperately to process what the doctor had said. All I heard in my head were the words "nothing more we can do for her." That phrase went 'round and 'round in my head.

Why did it have to be her? Why would God take her away from me? Who will I have when she's gone? Selena? If that's the case, I'm definitely on my own. There's no one else, just the selfish woman that gave birth to me but didn't want anything to do with me afterward.

I can't believe she had the nerve to come here and act like a loving, grieving daughter. She doesn't give a damn about Gram.

The entire time I'd watched the doctor give Selena the details about Gram's condition, her face had been sad, but the sadness hadn't reached her eyes. As far as I could tell, she'd never felt love for her mother or anyone else except herself.

I just couldn't understand why Selena hated Gram so much. I knew Gram had done everything she could for her daughter, but apparently it wasn't enough for Selena. Maybe it was because their life was so hard — things were different then. A single, bi-racial woman with a child was never going to have it easy.

It also didn't help that Selena had mental issues. Gram told me she was bipolar and that the symptoms manifested when she was fourteen. She was prescribed medication, but as she got older, she didn't want to take it. Without it, she was violent and uncontrollable.

At her wit's end, Gram turned to alcohol to dull the pain and cope. She fell into the bottle for a couple of years, and by the time she kicked the booze and straightened her life out, her daughter had become someone she didn't recognize.

By age sixteen, Selena was drinking, smoking pot, popping pills, and snorting coke with the best of them. It's amazing that she managed to survive at all. *I don't understand why she gets to live and Gram doesn't. Why is the one person who cares about me being taken from me?*

As I wallowed in my misery, I realized I heard music. I followed the sound, and it led me to Room 504. Whoever was playing and singing was talented. I looked on the white board the nurses always fill out with patient information, and it said Jonathan Parker.

The blinds were closed, and a handsome man was sitting in a wheelchair in the darkened room, playing guitar and singing. He was only a few years older than me, and wore a melancholy smile as he sang to the middle-aged couple sitting with him.

I slid down the wall to the floor and sat there in the hall, listening. I could feel the sorrow and hopelessness in his song, and I could relate. He was singing everything I felt.

"I know that it's hard, and it's breaking your hearts
Knowing that I cannot be here.
Just think of me happy, no longer in pain,
No worries, no doubts, and no fears.
Just think of me now,
Memorize this look on my face.
And know that I'm with you
With every breath, with every step that you take,
Just remember me as I am now."

The singing stopped, and I didn't even need to see anything else to know — the singer was saying his goodbyes.

I couldn't imagine facing death if things were reversed and my Gram had to be the one to let me go. It was odd, because this guy seemed to be okay with it. If I was in his position, I'd be mad at God, the world, and everyone in it. How the hell did he get to that place of acceptance? I'm not sure I could ever be that accepting of Gram's diagnosis and her inevitable death.

I was suddenly hit by everything that was happening in my life. I was numb, and at the same time the grief overwhelmed me. *Is this what I'll be feeling from now on? I don't know if I can stand it. What the hell am I going to do?*

I put my head between my legs, suddenly feeling lightheaded and claustrophobic. The walls of the hospital were closing in on me and I felt like all the oxygen had been sucked from the building. I sat like that, concentrating on taking one breath at a time until my heart finally stopped racing and that horrible claustrophobic feeling passed.

I heard a noise and looked up to see the beautiful hazel-green eyes of the handsome singer. Even though I knew he was sick, he was still the finest-looking guy I'd ever seen.

He stared at me like he could see right into my soul. *I have to leave before I make a scene and fall apart completely in front of this stranger,* I thought. I got to my feet as quickly as I could, with my arms and legs feeling like lead, and started to walk away.

"Wait! Don't leave."

I froze, but didn't turn around.

"I just want to talk to you. Please?"

I slowly turned around and saw how fragile he looked, sitting in the wheelchair. I knew it must have taken a lot out of him to wheel himself out into the hall, and I immediately felt bad. I walked back toward him and stopped about three feet away and just looked at him.

"What's your name?"

"Sky," I said, as a little thrill went through me because he was staring at me so intently with those beautiful eyes.

"That's a pretty name. My name's Jonathan. It's nice to meet you," he said in a formal way, offering to shake my hand.

"You, too," I said, as we shook. I felt guilty for intruding on what seemed like a private moment with his loved ones.

"What brings you here?"

"My Gram is down at the end of the hall," I responded, as the feeling of doom and utter panic came back full force.

Jonathan reached out and covered my hand with both of his. "It's going to be okay. Don't be scared."

"You don't know anything about it," I said with my head down, fighting tears.

"Look at me. Of course I do."

I looked into his eyes and realized he understood everything I was feeling. "You're right. I'm sorry."

"It's okay. How old are you?"

"Sixteen."

"Well, I'll let you in on a secret. At your age everything feels big and bad and insurmountable — but it's not. You have to push through, no matter what. You *will* make it to the other side."

"Is that what you do, push through?" I asked bitterly. "I heard you in there. It sounded like you were saying goodbye. You're not pushing through, so why should I?"

I saw an emotion flash across his face, and then he said, "Come to my room and talk to me for a while." He turned around and wheeled himself back to his room, then slowly got into bed.

"Would you all excuse us, please?" he asked the people waiting in his room when I followed him inside.

When they were completely out of earshot, he turned his attention back to me and said, "Well, go ahead and sit down and I'll tell you my story."

I got settled in the chair beside his bed, and he started talking. "I have a bad heart. Every day it gets worse and every day I get weaker. Hell, some days I can barely stand up. I know I'm going to lose my life, but what's worse than that is knowing my parents will lose everything too. They won't accept the fact that I'm going to die, and they mortgaged their house and took out loan after loan just to get me here — to a day I've been dreading.

"They've found a donor heart for me, but my survival rate is a whopping thirty percent. I have to go through with the transplant, because if I don't it will make everything they've done and all they've sacrificed mean nothing. So, I'm going to do it, even though someone else might have better odds of survival if they took the heart I'm going to receive.

"You don't know anything about real fear, hopelessness or tragedy. I know that song was the last one I'll ever sing, so yes, it was my goodbye."

"But—"

"No, let me talk. ... I'd trade your reality for mine, no matter what it is. You haven't lost everything, and you have your whole life ahead of you. You're hurting, but that won't last forever. It will fade with time. So, yes, you need to push through because you have the luxury of a life afterwards." He stopped then, tears rolling down his face.

"You know wanna how I feel about those statistics?" I asked angrily. "I think you're giving them too much power. No doctor can determine your path, only you and God have that power. Gram taught me that. I've never heard anyone as musically gifted as you. It would be a shame if the world lost you because you're not willing to survive.

"I know you're not done living yet. Everything you just told me proves it. This donor heart is a blessing, and it's for *you*, not someone else. You need to have faith. You have a family that loves you. I don't have that. I just have Gram, and I'm losing her. So, you *are* blessed. I know if it was in her power, Gram would *never* leave me. The people who love you are fighting for you, so you can't give up. It's in your power to stay with them. This is your life, your future, and you have to fight for it."

"I wish I had your faith, but I don't anymore. I don't think that everything will be okay, and I don't trust God's will."

"Well, I think you're an idiot."

"Can I ask you to do me a favor?"

"What is it?"

"I need to know why my song made you cry? I want to know if you think I could've had a career in music in another life."

"No. I won't answer your question."

"Really? Why not?"

"You want me to make it okay that you're leaving the people who love you, your talent, and your life behind. I won't do that.

I will *not* give you permission to die in peace without guilt. I believe you'll survive the surgery, and *you* need to believe it too.

"I'm doing this for purely selfish reasons. I need you to make it so I'll have at least one friend in this world. If you want to know the answer to your question, then stick around and find out. Prove those statistics wrong!"

"Look at me, Sky. As long as I'm breathing, you'll always have a friend, no matter what. Thank you for being tough with me. No one else has been brave enough to try to talk some sense into me. I think you're my guardian angel, and I'm going to fight to stick around so I can find out why you were sent to me. I think you've just saved my life, and hopefully one day I can return the favor. I'll see you soon, right?"

"You'd better," I say, fighting the tears running down my face.

"Okay, Angel. See you on the other side." He looked out the door and nodded to his parents and the nurses who were hovering in the background.

I watched as they prepped him for his heart transplant, then rolled him away. I suddenly realized my heart had been stolen by this handsome singer.

After his successful surgery, I went back to see Jonathan to check on his progress. He seemed to be doing well, and we exchanged addresses and phone numbers and promised to stay in touch. As weird as it was, this virtual stranger had become my trusted friend. It felt really good to know there was someone I could count on to be there when I needed a sympathetic ear.

***

Chapter 7

Gram died a week later, and her funeral was the following week. The day after, the reading of her will took place at her lawyer's offices not far from where we lived. Selena walked into that office with a huge smile on her face. I knew she thought she'd hit the jackpot. From that smug look on her face, no one would guess she'd just buried her mother.

Unfortunately for her, Gram had known she would use anything that was left to her to finance her various addictions, so she got nothing. Gram left the house to me — I would take possession when I turned eighteen. There was no mention of any money, so I assumed it all went to pay the hospital bills. The look on Selena's face when she heard I got the house was frightening, and I realized I'd have to keep my head down and watch out for her vengeance.

Her anger and selfishness were the reasons I would never think of her as my mom. Even in my thoughts, I always referred to her by her first name. It made me sad to think that someone as wonderful as Gram had been saddled with Selena as her daughter.

An hour before my work shift started a few days later, I got a call from Gram's lawyer asking me to come back to his office.

He told me I needed to come by myself and was extremely vague about why he wanted to see me. So, I called work and told them I'd be late, then caught a bus and went to see him.

When I got there, Mr. Banks apologized for his cloak and dagger meeting request. He said this was the way Gram had said it needed to be.

"To ensure there is no question as to how things have been handled, I'll be recording our meeting," he told me as I sat down in front of his desk.

He turned on the recorder, then picked up an envelope and continued, "This envelope contains Sabrina Walker's *complete* final will and testament. Helena Sky Walker, please state for the record that this envelope I am presenting to you is sealed and does not appear to have been tampered with."

"It's sealed and doesn't appear to be tampered with," I repeated for benefit of the recording after looking at the envelope.

"Go ahead and open it."

I broke the seal, unfold the document, and saw the pages had been handwritten by Gram. Just seeing her handwriting made me start crying. I quickly pulled myself together, because obviously Gram had some things to tell me. I took a deep breath and started reading:

> *I, Sabrina Walker, am of sound mind and am not acting under duress or undue influence. I fully understand the nature and extent of all my property and its disposition contained herein, and, do hereby declare this document to be my Last Will and Testament. This document revokes any and all other wills and codicils made by me.*

My Dearest Sky,

If you are reading this, I'm absent in the body, and present with my Lord. I'm going to miss you so much. I know you're probably sad, and I'm sorry for that, baby. I want you to know that the day I took you in was the best day of my life.

I found out I was sick right after I got custody of you. The cancer was Stage 2 then. I'd seen some of my friends deal with this very same illness, and it was the treatment that crippled them the most. You needed me, and I decided to keep my quality of life good for as long as possible — that meant no crazy treatments that would rob me of time with you. I chose you, baby girl.

You were my second chance — a chance to get things right. I tried and failed to raise your mother to be a beautiful person. But you, you're my greatest success.

I'm sorry I waited so long to tell you I was sick. I was in denial for a long time and I just couldn't face the fact that I'd have to leave you.

I need you to be okay, but I also need you to do something for me. I'm giving you the wisdom of my years, and the knowledge you'll need to face this next step. Do what I ask, so I can rest in peace.

Know that I always have your back, even now that I'm not there with you.

Here's what I need you to do:

Under no circumstances should you ever reveal this letter or second Will to your mother or anyone else. *The only exception to this is if you find some-one you trust and love with your whole heart.*

Don't draw any extra attention to yourself, especially from your mother or anyone she brings around. Find some friends, get a job and stay out of that house and away from her as much as possible. Eat there, sleep there, and that's it. I know this is probably coming off harsh, but I need you to sur-vive this, and survive her. Fade into the woodwork as much as you possibly can.

Focus, study your butt off, go to college and get the hell away from your mother. Don't look back — it's sink or swim time.

I've left our home to you, not Selena. My wish is for you to keep it as your safe haven. My dream is that one day you'll fill it with a family of your own. I'm just sad I won't be there to see that happen.

Don't be scared to make mistakes. I know you will, no matter how hard you try not to. Every-one makes mistakes. The most important thing is to learn from them. My biggest hope is that you find someone who loves you and will help you get through all of the hurt you're bound to go through.

When you do get away from Selena's influence, live, my precious baby girl. Go to college, study, have fun, pledge a sorority, find a boyfriend, fall in love. I don't care what you do with the money I'm leaving to you, but my wish is that some of it should pay for your college education. Knowledge is power, remember that.

Now, here's my final message. I want you to listen very carefully to what Mr. Banks has to say to you. He's going to need your undivided attention. He's going to help you hide what I'm leaving you so that Selena won't even know about it. You should never tell her about what you've learned today — nothing good will come of it if you do.

My sweet girl, I'm going to miss you so much. Know I love you with everything in me. Thank you for giving me a chance at redemption. I'm with you, always.

Ever Yours,
Gram

It took me an hour to sign everything and get the lawyer's instructions. Gram left me $150,000, in addition to the house. The funds would stay in a Wells Fargo account until I turned eighteen, and Mr. Banks would help manage everything for me.

It was so overwhelming that after I left the lawyer's office, I called my boss and told him I wasn't going to make it to work. Instead, I went to the same Wells Fargo bank where my funds were waiting and rented a safety deposit box so I could keep the documents I'd just received secret and safe, just like Gram instructed.

***

As time went by, I did exactly what Gram had told me to do, though I didn't have to worry about close friends or boyfriends because I didn't have either of those. I kept everyone at a distance. I pretended to hang out with people, study with them, go to the mall — all the regular stuff teenagers do — but in reality,

I was working as a cashier at a fast food restaurant. Whenever I wasn't working, I was studying my ass off.

I didn't have to worry about Selena finding out, because she just didn't care. She didn't know me well enough to know I was pretending. She just lived in my house for free and walked around resenting me because she knew if I called social services they would kick her out of my house and most likely grant me emancipation. The only reason I hadn't already tried that was my fear of what she'd do if I did.

So, I did my time, knowing I'd be out of high school soon — I was a junior — and off to college. I opened a savings account linked to the account Gram had set up for me, and I saved every penny possible from my job. Thank God, I was able to keep my job a secret from Selena, otherwise I'm positive she would've taken what I earned for herself.

It was hard adjusting to the lack of love and affection in my life after Gram was gone. Living with Selena was like living in hell. She barely acknowledged my existence. I guess living with her was better than being in some foster home or on the streets, but I definitely wanted to get away from her as soon as possible. Some people were just bad, and in my heart of hearts, I knew she was one of them. I was ashamed to be her daughter and constantly worried that one day I'd become just like her.

***

Eventually, all of my hard work, discipline, and dedication paid off. Mid-way through my senior year, I was accepted to all three of the out of state colleges I'd applied to, as well as Georgia State. After I considered everything, going to school out of state just seemed too overwhelming, so I decided on GSU.

I graduated with a perfect GPA and a full scholarship. The money I'd saved, combined with Gram's money, would mean I could get a small apartment near campus and live comfortably. I'd done it — I was finally going to get away from Selena! The only damper on my elation was realizing I'd have to find a way to get Selena out of my house.

I talked to Mr. Banks about this and he told me to let her know she'd have to move when I went off to school. If she didn't cooperate and move out, he would involve the police and have her evicted. I hoped it wouldn't come to that, but I just couldn't see Selena giving up a free place to stay without a fight. Mr. Banks assured me that he would take care of it for me if that happened, so I didn't worry too much about it.

He even offered to find a service to clean and close up the house so it would be ready and waiting for me when I decided to move back. I wasn't sure I'd ever do that, since the emotions connected to that house were so overwhelming. On one hand, there were the memories of Gram and everything I'd lost, and on the other there was what I'd gone through living with Selena for the last two years. I just couldn't deal with that, and my little college apartment seemed like the perfect place to be.

Chapter 8

The one constant in my life after Gram died and I was forced to live with Selena was Jonathan. After his successful surgery, he and I kept in touch, both with old-fashioned letters and a few calls here and there, because I didn't want to put a lot of money into my pre-paid phone. The letters seemed more intimate somehow, and it let us get to know each other really well.

I even had a secret nickname for him— JJ. No one but me got to call him that, and it made me feel special. Even though I was sad that we never got to see each other, just knowing he was there and would pay attention to everything I poured into my letters was enough.

While I was busy finishing high school, JJ was busy too. It was like he'd never been knocking on death's door, and in a short time, he'd become a star. The music world knew him as Jonah Parker, but to me, he'd always be my JJ.

Less than two years after his life-changing surgery, he was embarking on a US tour and I was excited to find out he was coming to my city. I planned to get a ticket to see the performance, because I could really use a friendly face right now — even if I was only seeing him from the concert floor.

When I got his latest letter, it included a front row VIP ticket and a backstage pass to the Atlanta concert. I don't know why I was surprised, since he was always extremely generous. I just knew that night was going to be epic!

I was right. The concert was amazing! JJ even sang the song I'd first heard at the hospital as his encore, and he dedicated it to his angel — me!

I was in awe as I followed one of the tour security guards to a private room backstage afterwards. We came to a door, and he scanned my backstage pass and escorted me to a TSA-style metal detector. After that, another security guy patted me down and went through my bag.

Once that was done, I was walking with yet another security guard who took me to a lavish room filled with fans and tons of people with badges hanging around their necks. There was even a table filled with all sorts of snacks, soft drinks and liquor of every kind. It was all a little overwhelming.

Since I didn't know anyone, I decided to find a corner where I could people-watch without being in the way. I spotted the perfect place, and as I turned to head in that direction, I stepped on someone's foot. I started to apologize and found myself staring into a pair of familiar green eyes.

JJ was wearing a black hoodie with the hood up so he could slip into the room unnoticed. No one else had realized who he was, but he couldn't fool me.

"I'm so sorry. I didn't see you there," I said, silently thanking God that my voice sounded normal.

"Why would you when there are so many interesting people to look at all crammed into one room?"

"Well, I came here tonight looking for one specific person."

He looked at me when I said this, and I swear I felt his eyes on me like a caress.

"Is that so?"

"It is."

"And just who would that lucky bastard be?" he asked, smiling and making my heart want to flutter out of my chest.

"Unfortunately, I stepped on his foot. He probably won't be too happy to see me now. It's a shame, because I've waited a long time to see him again."

"Let me assure you, he's not easily offended, and his toes are just fine."

"Well that's a relief."

"I'm glad you came."

"I'm so happy to be here. Thank you for the ticket and back-stage pass."

"Believe me, the pleasure is all mine. Sky, you look absolutely amazing," he said as he took my hand and looked into my eyes. "Let me put in an appearance, sign some autographs for fans and make sure I've made it worth it for the people who paid through the nose to be here, and then we'll go somewhere more private."

I felt like I was floating on cloud nine. I watched as he worked the room. He was really good with people. He gave each of them the attention they craved, without spending too much time doing it. It was interesting to see how everyone in the room adored him.

When he finally came over and took my hand so we could leave, I felt like my night was perfect. We went to his hotel room, ordered room service and talked for hours. Eventually, talking turned into kissing and more.

The next morning, I woke to JJ rushing around, packing his suitcase. All I wanted to do was lay there and bask in the glow of what we'd done the night before. Seeing that he was getting ready to leave was disappointing.

"What time is your plane?" I asked as I got out of bed.

"I've only got an hour and a half to get packed and get to the airport. Sorry, I really wish we had more time. You can stay and order room service and enjoy the room for a little while longer if you want."

"Thanks, but it won't be the same without you here."

"Again, I'm sorry. My manager doesn't really ever leave me any time for myself. She says I have to work extra hard if I want to be a legend — that's really more her dream than mine though."

"You're already a star, at least as far as I'm concerned," I said and nudged his arm playfully.

"You're so cute, but I've gotta get going. I left the address for the next tour stop on the table over there. Write to me?"

"You know I will."

He grabbed me and kissed me until my toes curled, then he was gone.

I stayed and ordered room service. It was nice to feel pampered and pretend I was rich for a little while. All too soon, I'd have to go back to my poor girl life, so I enjoyed every minute of it.

I wrote to JJ at the address he'd given me as soon as I got back home. I poured out all of my feelings and made sure he knew how special our night together had been for me. I dropped the letter in the mail that afternoon and eagerly waited for his response.

***

JJ's next letter took forever to get to me and it was really short. He didn't comment on our night together or anything I'd said in my last letter, he just talked about how busy he was and how the tour was going. It was a little worrying that he didn't really include anything personal this time, but I thought maybe someone was reading over his shoulder or something and he didn't want to include anything he thought I wouldn't want others to know.

So, my next letter to him was as personal, passionate and heartfelt as the last one. I just knew he'd respond in kind with his next note.

I waited for three weeks, but no letter came. Just when I'd decided my letter to him had gotten lost in the mail, I finally heard from him. This note was even shorter than the last one, and it was so impersonal that I burst into tears after I read it. It was clear he wasn't interested in expanding our relationship — it was also starting to sink in that he didn't want anything else to do with me.

Before that wonderful night we spent together, he'd been like my own personal prince charming. The fact that he was a rock star and I was a nobody hadn't seemed to matter to him. I guess I only saw what I wanted to see. In reality, he was just like all of those celebrities I read about in the tabloids. I gave him my virginity because he had my heart, and he took it without a second thought. What an entitled asshole! How could I have been so blind?

I buried my head in my pillow and cried until I fell asleep. When I woke up, I felt horrible. My head hurt, my eyes were swollen and I felt like I was going to puke. How could I have been so naïve?

After my sad revelation, I went back to my boring life of working and going to school. I felt like a zombie and couldn't make myself care about anything. I didn't want to eat, in fact I felt like I was going to barf every time I even thought about eating anything more than toast or crackers. I was miserable and felt like I was completely alone in the world.

I didn't write another letter to JJ and I didn't hear from him again. Apparently, I wasn't on his mind at all. That irrefutable fact made me cry every time it crossed my mind, so I promised myself I just wouldn't think about him anymore.

***

Two months later, when I was standing in front of my bathroom counter holding a positive pregnancy test, I had no choice but to think of JJ. *How could I have been so stupid?* I berated myself. I knew about birth control, but in the heat of the moment, we hadn't used any. *Nothing like paying for one mistake for the rest of my life. I can't raise a baby — it's all I can do to take care of myself. What kind of mother would I be? How can I even consider having a baby when my biological mother is such a monster? I love this child already, so there's no way I'd even consider abortion. Guess I'd better find out how adoption works so I can ensure that he or she gets good, loving parents who want a child.*

I decided to tell JJ about the baby and what I planned to do. He had rights too, so I contacted his manager to see if I could get his phone number or a current address — the cell number he'd given me had been out of service for a while now. His manager, Nicole, gave me an address and said me she wasn't allowed to give out his cell number.

I wrote him a letter and awaited his response with trepidation. When I didn't hear from him, I sent another letter. I waited and waited, but he never wrote back or called. Apparently, he truly didn't want anything to do with me — with *us*. So, I hardened my heart and did what was needed to ensure my child would have good parents and a better chance in life than I could provide.

I couldn't give up writing to JJ, even though I knew who and what he was. Writing those letters made me feel better, like I wasn't completely alone. I knew it was stupid, but I needed every little "good" thing I could find. So, I bought a cheesy decorated box on closeout and used it to hold the letters I wrote to him but never sent.

A few months later, I realized my letter therapy wasn't really helping me anymore. Each letter was angrier and more hurt-filled than the last, and I no longer felt better when I signed them and added them to the box. The truth was shining through to me, finally, and I had become bitter and filled with self-pity.

This has to stop! I thought as the realization hit me full in the face. *I will not waste my life pining for someone who doesn't care about me. I'm taking charge and doing what's best for me and my baby. No more fantasies. I made a stupid mistake, and my child and I have to live with the consequences. Time to quit feeling sorry for myself and start living in the real world.*

From that moment forward, I made a conscious effort to remove JJ from my life. My only thoughts were about the future and what it held for me. I removed emotion from the equation and let my ambition be my guide.

I came back to the present, filled with sadness over what had and hadn't been. Now, after all this time, he had come back into my life. I hadn't spoken to him in person since that fateful night, and I wasn't sure how I was going to handle this meeting. *Will I be able to guard my heart and keep all of the emotions from the past bottled up inside?*

Chapter 9

G ram had taught me to always look at the bigger picture and be a champion for others, even when it cost me personally. She practiced what she preached too. Even after she was gone, she managed to do something my own mother wouldn't do — she put me first. It was like her spirit was always there, looking out for me. Memories of her were a comfort to me in my darkest hours, so I always tried to emulate her.

At times, I wonder what Gram would think of the woman I've become. Would she be proud? Would she approve of my choices? What would she have to say about my relationships with Ash and Alex? It made me sad to realize I'd never know the answers to those questions. I missed her advice more than anything. She never made me feel stupid, she just told me what I needed to know.

More than anything I wish I could tell her about JJ — how he made me feel and how I wished we could have had more. I'd also ask her if I put up with Ash because JJ made me feel like I wasn't worthy of anyone better. JJ was my first love, and my heart still sinks when I think of him and everything I lost.

This meeting has really woken up the ghosts of the past. What if he recognizes me? What if he doesn't? How can I act normal around this man, the only one I've ever truly loved?

JJ is worse than a ghost that refuses to stop tormenting me. The thought of him is a threat to my very sanity. Reality intruded on my thoughts, and I realized that in a little while he's going to be right here in front of me. I'm torn between excitement and dread.

One thing's for sure. I'm going to look like a million bucks at this meeting, I thought with resolve. I managed to get an appointment for a fresh silk press for my hair and a full body wax. Next came makeup, nails and wardrobe. *What I wear has to say I am the HBIC, and I have arrived,* I thought as I pulled into my driveway at exactly 7:55 p.m.

Entering Gram's house — my house now — always gave me a warm feeling. I couldn't imagine living anywhere else. *Lord knows, I need the calming effect of home right now,* I thought as I walked through the kitchen. I glanced at the clock and saw I needed to get a move on or I'd be late.

I hurried to change, and after what seemed like hours of primping, I was finally a finished masterpiece. I decided to leave right away, so I would get there early. *JJ may have set the time and place, but this is my show.*

I pulled into the hotel's valet parking at exactly at 8:30 p.m. I glanced into the mirror one last time before grabbing my briefcase, stepping out, and handing the keys to the valet. I smiled to myself, knowing that Mr. Jonathan Jonah Parker wasn't going to know what the hell hit him.

I could tell JJ resented the fact that I knew about his transplant and had the nerve to guilt trip him. *I have to remember he isn't my sweet JJ anymore,* I thought. *Chances are, he won't even realize who I am. I don't think I really want him to, either.*

51

As the elevator whisked me to the top floor, I realized I'd come to this meeting thinking I'd get JJ out of my system once and for all so I could truly put the past behind me. But now, all I felt was excitement about seeing him again. *That man left scars on my heart that have never healed,* I realized with dismay.

I left behind the beautiful view of downtown Atlanta as I exited the glass elevator and walked to the hostess podium. When I inquired about a reservation for Parker, she smiled, and said, "Right this way. He's expecting you." *Damn! So much for being early.*

She led me to the most private part of the restaurant, and we stopped at an empty table. "He was just here," she said, looking flustered.

"It's fine. Thank you."

I seated myself and picked up a menu so I'd have something to do with my hands. I saw movement out of the corner of my eye, and when I turned, there was JJ walking toward me. The closer he got, the louder my heart pounded. This felt like a dream. I never expected to be this affected by just seeing him again, and I can't think of one thing to say. *So much for this being my show.*

"You're the president, huh?" he asked, totally unimpressed.

"It's an honor to meet you, Mr. Parker," I stammered, putting on the most stunning, non-terrified smile I could summon. *He's just as beautiful as I remembered,* I think, struggling to keep from drooling. *He hasn't really changed, even after all these years.* It's all I can do to keep from fantasizing about him right this moment.

"I'm sorry, you aren't the person I expected to meet," he said, looking confused.

I smile, knowing the Foundation's website has pictures of all staff and officers — except me. The former president's photo is still online. It's not public knowledge that she's under investigation for embezzling, so for now no one knows her position has been filled by me. The marketing department decided it was best to leave her picture up until the investigation finished up.

The former president was no Shrek, but she wasn't exactly fine either. *At least he went to the trouble of doing a little research before our meeting.* "Please, have a seat. Let's begin our meeting, shall we? I can always show you my driver's license if you need to verify my identity," I quip, with just the right amount of sarcasm.

He quickly recovered, smiled, and sat down. Once he was seated, I pulled out the paperwork I brought with me, then looked to see that I had his attention.

"I'll get straight to the point, because I don't want to take up too much of your time. The Good Samaritan's Foundation would like to work with you on a five-month fundraising project. The Foundation wants to fund the medical care for three carefully selected candidates who have desperate needs. All three candidates are students who have received scholarships from top schools in the country. They have bright futures ahead of them, but only if they receive the help they need from us.

"The first candidate is Adrianna Pierce. She's a talented ballerina with an impressive GPA. She's been accepted to Julliard School of Arts with a full scholarship. Adrianna has been diagnosed with stage IB cervical cancer and is currently in palliative care, which is a specialized type of medical care for people living with serious illnesses. Her cancer was caught early and is treatable, but the treatments are expensive.

"Next, we have Rachelle Kennedy, an Elite Scholars student who is also a talented violinist. She has been accepted to Curtis Institute of Music in Pennsylvania. Rachelle has acute lymphoblastic leukemia, and is receiving treatment right now, since it's crucial to treat this disease quickly to increase her chance of remission and possible cure. The treatments' costs are prohibitive and lack of funds threatens her future almost as much as the disease.

"Finally, there's Elijah Redmond, a high school senior. He's captain of his school's football and soccer teams, and has a full football scholarship to Georgia State University. Elijah was on his way to meet friends at a party but never made it because his vehicle was t-boned by a drunk driver. As a result of his injuries, he is now a paraplegic. Tests conducted by our team have determined there's a very good chance this paralysis can be reversed with treatment that includes surgery and aggressive therapy. Again, these treatments are extremely expensive and his family cannot afford them.

"All three of these candidates have a good chance of responding well to their recommended treatments, but that can only happen if the Foundation can find the funds to help them with expenses. It would be a crime to let a lack of funding deny these children their amazing futures. Time is their enemy," I concluded dramatically, and then looked at him in a way I hoped would motivate him to work with us.

"I can see you're passionate about this cause," he said when I finished. "Will you still give these children what they need, even if I don't decide to work with you?"

"To be frank, we don't have the funding available to do that right now. The Foundation had a recent management shakeup and there's an internal investigation that hasn't been made public yet that has frozen our assets. Until that investigation is complete, the Foundation can't move forward without additional funding sources.

"Despite this setback, we're still trying to carry out our mission. If you decide to work with us, you'd most likely be setting us up to help others in the future. Having you on-board will not only alleviate our funding issues, it will also give other investors a renewed sense of confidence in what we're trying to do so they're join us in our efforts."

"What have you promised these kids?"

"We haven't promised them anything, but we have hinted that we can help them."

"Fine," he said, sighing with resignation. "Tell me about what you want from me."

"Okay. If you don't mind, I'm going to read it from the contract we've prepared for you."

"Feeling a little overconfident, aren't we *Ms. President?*" he asked with a bit of venom in his voice.

"Not at all, I just believe in being prepared. So, we're proposing a five-month working relationship with you. The mission of this relationship will be to raise funds for the three children we just discussed. This fundraising will be accomplished by you performing four concerts, one for each child, and a final concert that will earn funds for future Foundation recipients. The first three concerts will be small venue, intimate concerts that can command high ticket prices from wealthier concert-goers, and the fourth concert will be an arena event that's geared more toward the general public.

"The proceeds from these events will be used exclusively to fund treatment and therapy for children the Foundation sponsors. That's it in a nutshell. What do you think?"

He leaned back in his seat, wearing an odd look on his face. "That's it?"

"Yes, that's it. I won't take up any more of your time. You can think it over and get back to me," I said quickly, hoping to leave before I do or say something stupid. "I can be reached directly at the number you called earlier. Please let me know if you have any questions. I'd also be happy to forward the formal proposal to your lawyers if you like. Please don't take too long to decide. As I said, time is our enemy here. It was a pleasure to meet you," I said, gathering my things to leave.

"Don't I get to ask questions?"

"I'm sorry. I thought things were pretty straightforward. Please, feel free to ask anything you like."

"First, I thought this was a dinner meeting. Aren't we going to have dinner?"

"It is, yes. After our brief conversation on the phone this morning, I just thought you'd prefer to get straight to the point without having to sit through dinner with me."

"Well, do you have somewhere else to be?"

"Not at the moment."

"Have you eaten?"

"No, I haven't."

"Well, Ms. President, I say we have some dinner." He signaled a server and gave me a look I could only interpret as "game on."

The meal started out in an uncomfortable way, but eventually the conversation began to flow naturally. This shouldn't have been a surprise to me, since JJ had never been difficult to talk to. What did surprise me was I liked him. I had been prepared to dislike the superstar, mega-rich version of JJ, but the more we talked the more I found myself drawn to him.

"So, is there a Mr. President?"

"Why would you want to know that?"

"Just making conversation."

"Ah, no," I answered, trying my best to hide my smile.

"Is that by choice?"

"Maybe. I'd ask about your love life if it weren't something I could look up in the tabloids or on Instagram."

"Ouch!"

"That was rude. Sorry."

"Don't apologize for being honest. You're right, I am a one hundred percent certified playboy bachelor. But, I'm more private than you think. What you see in the press isn't really me — that's my celebrity twin. I'm a completely different person," he said, flashing a sexy smile.

"If you say so," I said, smiling back at him and cringing inside because I could see a glimmer of the boy I used to know — the one who had inspired me to help others. Sadly, I know it's actually just an illusion.

His earlier question about a Mr. President lingered in the back of my mind. *Will I always be just a career woman? I'm not exactly girlfriend material or brimming with maternal instincts, and I certainly don't want to turn out like my mother.* I hated this internal monologue, because I knew where it would lead me. These feelings are part of the reason I gave up the most precious thing in my life — my baby girl.

"Penny for your thoughts," he said, bringing me back to the here and now.

"Trust me, they're nothing that would interest you. I want to hear more about the infamous Jonah Parker," I said, trying to divert his attention away from me.

"Oh no, it's your turn. I want to know how you came to hold the prestigious Ms. President title. I also want to know how you knew about my past and my medical history — that's not something you read about in the tabloids."

I looked up, startled by the intense look he was directing my way. "I can't reveal my sources," I said, avoiding his eyes by studying my plate.

"I figured you wouldn't tell me, but it was worth a try."

That's a relief! I've never been a good liar, and I always keep my past and my real identity to myself. That's not really lying, it's just not revealing everything.

Before I know it, the restaurant is closing. It's like we've been in our own little bubble where nothing from the outside world could interrupt our time together. I know for a fact that neither of us wants the evening to end, but as I know so very well — all good things always come to an end. *Just be happy you've had this time with him and let it go at that,* I chide myself when I find I'm wishing for more.

"So, are we on a first-name basis yet?" Jonah asked as we walked out of the restaurant and he looped his arm in mine.

"Why would you think that?" I asked, looking at him as we step off the elevator.

"Well, I've spilled everything but blood for you tonight, so I figured I should at least be able to call you by your first name."

He has a point. What could it hurt if he knows my name. He was the only one other than Gram who ever called me Sky, so there's no way anyone else can make the connection between Lena and Sky for him.

"Well, when you put it that way..." I paused, making him wait.

"So, it's settled. No more Mr. Parker; I'm Jonah. And you, Ms. President...?"

"My name is Lena."

We step up to the valet's station and I hand over my ticket. While we wait for my car, Jonah looks down at me with such an intense gaze it gives me pause.

"Tell me something, Lena. Have we met before?"

Shit! Stay cool. You've got this. "We hardly run in the same circles. Why would you think that?"

"I just— I feel like I know you from somewhere. I can't explain it, but I feel a pull toward you that I've only felt with one other person," he said as his eyes searched my face.

Does he know? "This person was a woman?"

"Yes, she—" He stopped and shook his head. "I haven't thought about her in a very long time. I don't know why she's suddenly on my mind now."

"Well, don't go digging up skeletons on my account, but I'd say it sounds like you have some unresolved feelings. If you want, you can tell me about her."

"I don't know. Honestly, I put her out of my mind years ago because I started to think I imagined her."

"That must be *some* imagination you have if your feelings are still this strong. I'll be the judge of your imagination theory. Tell me about her," I asked, floored that he thinks I wasn't real.

"The first time we met, Sky was just sixteen and I was in a really bad place. She listened outside my hospital room while I was singing to my parents. It was my last song before the surgery. I was saying goodbye to them because I was convinced I would die on the operating table. She changed my thinking that day, and if she hadn't been there, I doubt I would have made it off that table. She was my angel," he said, a small smile appearing on his beautiful face.

"We stayed in contact after that, but didn't see each other in person again until she came to one of my concerts. She was beautiful inside and out. We had a memorable night, and I was looking forward to many more, but unfortunately I didn't tell her that. I had to leave on tour the next morning, and then I got busy and didn't write much. Then, she just stopped writing to me all of the sudden and I never heard from her again. I wrote to her a couple of times to see what as wrong, but she didn't answer and I finally had to face the fact that she was never going to. My manager insisted she had probably been infatuated with me but had moved on once she satisfied her curiosity."

"Why did you give up so easily?"

"I figured I wasn't what she'd imagined after our night together, that or maybe she found some local guy and fell in love. So, I left well enough alone."

I almost forgot to breathe when I heard him say this. *He looks so conflicted. I thought he'd forgotten me. That I didn't mean anything to him. After all, I was just a silly teenager and he was a rock star.* I suddenly realized I'd had it wrong, because his expression said it all.

To be honest, it scared me and strengthened my resolve to make sure he never found out who I really was. *Sky's gone — dead and buried — and she isn't coming back. Sky is damaged. Sky is broken and filled with grief and pain. I can't handle being her ever again, and I certainly can't bear being hurt by him again.*

Chapter 10

I suddenly realize I'm standing beside my car having a mental meltdown in public. *I can't let this man undo everything I've worked so hard for. I've got to get out of here.* "She certainly sounds like a special person. I"m sorry it didn't work out for you. Thank you for a pleasant evening," I said, hurrying to open my car door. "I'll wait to hear from you or your lawyers."

"Don't leave yet. I know this sounds weird, but from the moment I saw you tonight, you took my breath away. It's like I'd been waiting for you without knowing it. Don't you feel it too?"

"I'm flattered. But, no, I don't."

"It's funny, I came here thinking you were the worst kind of person — someone who would lie, cheat, steal and manipulate to get what you want. But, you're nothing like that. For the first time tonight, though, I'm positive you're lying to me. So, let's put my theory to the test," he said right before his lips meet mine. Suddenly we were holding each other and kissing like our lives depended on it.

He pulled away, looked into my eyes, and my heart started beating so fast I wasn't sure if I was turned on or about to have a panic attack. I knew he was trying to make me acknowledge I felt something between us, but that would be my undoing. For me, he was like the drug addiction I'd kicked years ago, and suddenly someone was offering me a big hit. *I can't believe I let this happen,* I think as my brain tries its best to come back online.

"Hey, look at me," Jonah said. "I know you feel something. You want me. I can tell, so don't bother trying to deny it. I'm patient and I don't give up easily. Eventually you'll have to give in and admit it. Think about me when you're lying in bed alone tonight," he said as he opened my car door for me.

I didn't say anything, because I didn't trust myself. I just closed my door, started my car and drove away. I couldn't help myself, though. I watched him in the rear-view mirror until he was out of sight.

The whole drive home, I kept reliving that kiss. Just thinking about it made me want him. The way he looked at me, it was like I was the only woman in the world. The drive home was a blur of conflicting emotions, alternating with more thoughts of that damn kiss.

What the hell just happened? Is this some cosmic joke? The one man I've loved for all these years wants me, and I told him I'm not interested. WTF?

Shit, this is a mess! He hasn't agreed to anything with the Foundation yet, but I'm sure he will if he thinks he can get closer to me. I don't know if I can deal with him doing that. I mean, just a few hours ago I forgot to breathe when he said my name.

He's nothing like what I imagined. He's intelligent, vital and serious and he doesn't act like a celebrity at all. I can't help but compare him to the other men I've known and none of them come close, especially Ash.

I suddenly realize the only thing I feel for Ash, the man who was able to make me stop longing for JJ, is disgust. That makes me kind of sad. *Poor dorky Ash. He wasn't particularly handsome or athletic, and he didn't have much stamina, but I thought I loved him. All of those years I spent hiding in his shadow — what a waste.*

My brain switched gears in mid-stream and I was back to thinking about JJ. *What if seeing him after all these years was fate? Whatever it is, I need to keep my head and hold onto my panties around him. I have to find a way to distance myself emotionally or I'm going to be in trouble.*

I got the feeling that distancing myself was going to be difficult. *He seemed to take it as a direct challenge when I told him I didn't feel anything for him. Now he's the hunter and I'm prey. That's not the position I like to find myself in.* Even though I know how bad things could get for me, I'm still happy because he wants me. *I'm going to have to start working on my poker face. People have always told me that my facial expressions give me away.*

Well, I feel like shit. Damn dreams, I grouse to myself the next morning as I try to jump-start my foggy brain. *I haven't had a night like that in years. The last time it happened was after I gave my baby up for adoption. Stupid man — he has to come along and turn things upside down just when I finally have my shit together.*

Deep down, I know things can never truly be real between Jonah and me until I come clean about everything — and I can't do that! Plus, do I really want to get into another relationship and have to give up everything I've worked so hard for? *Why did I ever agree to contact him?*

Stop it! He hasn't said anything about a relationship. He's just interested in sex. Besides, true emotions are not his thing. I smile at this realization, and some of the tension leaves my body.

"Ugh! Get out of bed and get yourself ready for work. It's useless to lay here and worry about things that aren't real, and might never happen," I told myself.

I finally made it to the office, and I'm not even that late. I immediately sat at my desk and started looking at my schedule for the day.

"Good morning!" my boss Susan chirps, as she walks in without knocking.

"Good morning. How are you?"

"I'm great, but you look like you didn't get much sleep last night."

"Guilty."

"I come bearing good news. … You did it!"

"Did what?" I asked, as my heart dropped.

"You got him! I just had a call from Mr. Jonah Parker himself — not one of his people — him. He agreed to the proposal, with a few conditions. He and his lawyer will be here Monday to nail everything down. You're available, right?"

"Yes, of course. I'll be there."

"Great! We're so proud of you. And, as a bonus, the investors who were on the fence will surely be happy too. It probably wasn't easy to get him to agree, so as part of your reward for a job well done, I'm giving you the rest of the day off. Enjoy it, because you probably won't get another one until this project is finished. I'll handle anything you had going on today, so don't worry about that.

"I also booked a spa treatment for you a Spa-la-la. I get their deluxe treatment once a month, and it's a life saver! Enjoy your free day, and come back ready to work like a dog!" she said as she walked out the door.

Damn, I really hoped he'd turn it down. I'm both terrified and intrigued by the possibilities this opens up. Maybe I can reconcile the sweet JJ I knew years ago and the guarded man I had dinner last night.

I'm going to need all the peace and relaxation I can get to make it through this project, so I'm definitely heading to that spa with the stupid name, I think as I grab my stuff, tell Veronica I'm leaving for the day and head to my car.

Moments after Susan left Lena's office, she walked right past Mr. Jonah Parker. She quickly changed direction so she could see what he was up to. She came around the corner just as he walked up to Veronica's desk.

"Hi. May I—" Veronica stopped cold, and her eyes glazed over the moment she recognized him.

"Mr. Parker, I am a *huge* fan. I love your music. I—"

"Thank you, I appreciate that," he said, giving her a tight smile that said he wasn't thrilled to be fawned over.

"Oh, I could give you *way* more to appreciate than—"

"Actually, I'm here to see the president. Is she available?"

"No, she's not. In fact, she had an unfortunate accident, and she's not feeling well," Veronica said petulantly. "She left early. I could give her a message if you like."

"That would be great. Thanks."

"Okay, just write your message, name and number here, and I'll be sure to get it to her."

"Thank you," he said as he scribbled a short note.

"It's my *pleasure*, Mr. Parker."

Susan cringed at Victoria's blatant come-on.

Jonah gave her another tight smile and walked back in the direction he'd just come from.

Susan watched as Veronica took out her phone, snapped a picture of the note, then ripped it up and tossed it in the trash. *I've seen enough, and will deal with her later,* she thought as she turned and hurried to catch up with Jonah.

"Mr. Parker, is that you?" she called down the hall. "We spoke earlier today. I'm Susan McKinley," she said as she rushed to catch up with him. "I would've scheduled a tour if I'd known you were planning to stop in today," she said, flashing him a bright smile.

"It's a pleasure to meet you, Ms. McKinley. I don't need a tour. It was kind of a last-minute decision to stop by," he said, extending his hand.

Susan ignored it, and pulled him in for a hug. "I'm a hugger," she said by way of explanation, as she noted his startled expression. "Welcome to The Good Samaritan's Foundation."

"Thank you."

"You're welcome. Is there anything I can help you with?"

"Uh, no. I came by to speak to Ms. Walker. I was told she's not feeling well."

"Uh, yes. Ms. Walker did take a personal day. Was she expecting you?"

"No, she wasn't."

"Okay then. I'd really like to have a word with you in my office if you've got a minute. It won't take long."

***

Chapter 11

Lena pulled into her driveway that evening, feeling relaxed after her spa day. She felt completely at peace, until she saw who was waiting for her as she got out of her car — Jonah fucking Parker.

"Nice wheels, Ms. President."

"Why thank you. Not as nice as that red Lamborghini you used to drive though."

He paused, and I realized my mistake immediately. *That's the car he sent me a picture of in one of his letters.*

He smiled slowly, looking like a little kid at Christmas, and said, "I still bring her out from time to time. She's my baby. How do you know so much about me? Are you a fan?"

"Actually, yes. I researched you before suggesting we work together."

"Of course. Ever the thorough executive," he said with a smirk. "By the way, where have you been all day? Are you okay? I stopped by your office today and your assistant said you had some kind of accident and weren't feeling well, so I brought you some soup."

Veronica is so fired! "The soup was thoughtful but, as you can see, I'm not sick. My boss treated me to a spa day because I've been working a lot of hours. Did you need something else while you're here? Clarification of the proposal, maybe? … Wait, how did you get my address?"

"Trust me, you are *not* the only one who does their research and has connections. I had to do my homework before I considered working with a group that could have an impact on my professional reputation."

"Well, I'm glad you're so hands-on with your image. By the way, I was surprised to hear you've accepted the Foundation's proposal. You gave me the impression hell would freeze over before that happened. What changed your mind?"

"Let's just say your boss Susan is very persuasive. Aren't you going to invite me inside?"

"Do I have a choice?" I asked, fuming.

"There is always a choice. Though, I'm sure the Foundation would hate to hear you refused to invite a new partner and fundraiser into your home. Especially if he only wanted to make sure you were well after hearing you were ill. They'd probably want you to show some southern hospitality and address any concerns he might have. Right?"

I can't help but smile at his blatant manipulation I'm not in the mood to argue and the interior of the house is moderately put together, so I decide what the hell.

"Come on in," I said as I unlocked the front door.

The smile he flashed me was panty-melting. He followed me inside, and when I turned toward him I was left breathless once again. *I never in my life imagined Jonah "JJ" Parker would be standing in my entryway looking as scrumptious as a big piece of chocolate cake. I'm doomed!*

I quickly turned around and walked toward the kitchen, while desperately wracking my brain for what to do with him now that he's here. I go to the refrigerator and pull out my favorite cupcake Moscato, pluck two wine glasses from the cabinet and pour us each a glass.

"So, do you live here alone?" he asked from directly behind me.

How the hell did he sneak up on me like that? He's so close I can feel his body heat. One step back and I'd bump right into his happy place...

"Hello? Earth to Lena..."

"Oh, sorry. Yes, it's just me."

"Personal preference?"

"Yes, and no. I have no kids, no significant other and no family to speak of. So, it's just me." I realized that sounded pretty pathetic after I said it. I decided it was a good idea to put some space between us, so I moved over to the living room and sat down on the couch.

"Well, you have your Foundation to keep you company. As long as you have that, then you don't need anything or anyone else, right?" he asked as he picked up his glass and followed me. Instead of sitting down though, he decided to give himself a tour of the personal items dotting the room.

I did my best to remain calm and sip my wine while he does this. There isn't much to find, since most of my pictures from when I was young have been packed away. However, my diplomas are visible, and I am praying he doesn't look too hard at them, since they include my middle name.

A couple of minutes later, sat down on the opposite end of the couch.

"Did you enjoy your little uninvited tour of my things?" I asked, trying to keep my tone light and upbeat.

"We both know I'd probably be dead before you ever willingly gave me a tour," he said, wearing his trademark smirk.

"What do you want, Jonah?" I asked, my voice cold and suspicious. There are so many emotions swirling around inside me that all I can do is pick up my wine glass, chug, and wait for him to answer.

"You must have one hell of a Realtor to find this place so quickly. Did you rent it completely furnished?" he asked, still taking everything in.

"I didn't rent it, I own it. I had it renovated before I moved in. I designed the interior myself, so I'm glad you approve." I looked up to see a confused frown on his handsome face.

"What?" I asked, starting to panic.

"I'm just thinking. The timeline you gave me last night suggested you had very little time to find something once you accepted your job. How did you manage to buy a house, have it renovated, and decorate it yourself?"

Wow. This guy is really something, and he remembers details. I need to proceed with caution. "Okay, Mr. Nosy-pants. If I satisfy your ridiculous amount of curiosity, will you quit with the interrogation?"

"Sure, as long as I feel like you're being truthful."

"Okay. I was gifted this house years ago by someone very special to me. After college, I moved to Seattle with my boyfriend instead of coming back here. I stayed in Seattle while I got my doctorate and worked there for a little while after that. During that time, the property just sat here waiting for me to come back." I paused and poured myself another glass of wine. Thankfully, he didn't comment on my glass being empty already.

"Once I decided I was moving back, my friend referred me to a contractor who gave me appraisals and information about what updates the house needed. The structural renovations were minimal, and he was done in under three weeks," I finished and took a large drink of my second glass of wine.

"While all of the renovation work was going on, I was in Seattle tying up loose ends. The contractor had his work completed by the time I got here. The little bit of furniture that was here was run down, so I got rid of most of it and bought new. It was delivered and set up quickly, and my house was complete. Any more questions?"

"Yes. Are you rich?"

I couldn't help it, I fell back on the couch laughing. I looked at his face, and saw he was serious, and then I laughed even harder. Tears were running down my face by the time I could finally talk without laughing.

"Why would you think I'm rich?"

"Getting all of that done in that time frame? Plus, the expenses of travel and moving from across the country? Either you have some really good connections or you're rich. Which is it?"

"None of your damn business," I bark, irritated by his presumptuous attitude.

"You agreed to answer my questions. So, how *did* you pay for this? Did this *friend* cover the bill?" he asked, his implication clear.

"Get the fuck out of my house!" I yell, not caring about my job or anything else at the moment. *I refuse to explain myself to this entitled ass, and I will not back down. Who the hell does he think he is showing up like this and demanding answers to questions that are none of his damn business? How dare he question my character!*

Instead of leaving, he slid over and grasped my arms. "Lena, look at me."

I push him away and stand. "Don't fucking touch me! Who the fuck do you think you are? You bully your way into my home, demand explanations about how I live my life, and then make accusations as if you know me? You do *not* know me, and I won't allow you to disparage my character!

"Just because you're accustomed to all forms of rich, selfish, money hungry bitches does *not* mean that I'm a gold-digger who lets her friends pay her way through life. I've worked damned hard for every fucking thing I have! So, fuck you! *Now, get out!*" I was so furious at this point I couldn't even look at him.

"I was wrong for the way I phrased my question, but that's all I'm apologizing for. Why can't I get to know you better? Who is Lena, and why did she choose to be here and go to work for a barely credible foundation? Why does this mean so much to you? Why can't I find anything out about you, no matter where I look? What are you hiding, Lena?"

"You need to go," I say quietly.

"Yes, I guess I do," he said, setting down his wine glass, glaring at me and then heading out the door.

Chapter 12

The next morning, my alarm is driving daggers through my skull as it beeps insistently. I swipe at it, trying to shut if off without moving too much so my head doesn't explode. *I should not have finished off that bottle of wine last night. Today is doomsday and I'm not prepared at all. I have to get my shit together and look like the president at the meeting this morning, and I'm not sure how I'm going to pull that off with Jonah, my boss and the board sitting there staring at me.*

Maybe I can call in sick? Susan can handle it without me. No, I can't do that. This is my professional reputation on the line. I'm just going to have to suck it up and act like an adult.

I can't stop thinking of the look he gave me as he was leaving last night. It was a look that said, "This is war!" I just don't know whether he's going to be angry and vindictive because I threw him out or if he'll try to hunt me down and learn all of my secrets.

He's just going to have to understand that I can't deal with opening up to him. It's bad for my career and even worse, I think, for my mental health. There are some secrets that need to remain buried.

Part of me is thrilled that he's attracted to me, but I'm also terrified that some mannerism or familiar phrase is going to put the pieces together for him. *Come on, Lena. Get your head on straight and quit being so weak! You can't lose everything just because he likes you — you're not a teenager anymore. The Foundation is moving forward with Jonah no matter what, so just suck it up and stick to business.*

Three hours later, I marched my ass into the meeting with new resolve. I'll just let the board take the lead and keep my mouth shut.

This strategy was working well, until thirty minutes into the meeting when Jonah's lawyer began to explain the conditions that had to be met before Jonah would agree to participate. "The first condition is that Mr. Parker has the right to choose who he will work with for each event, and that person must agree to work with him and sign an NDA," the lawyer began.

"Second, Mr. Parker will be apprised of and have veto power over all promotions, as well as any and all decisions involving this project.

"Third, Mr. Parker requires that the person he works with for each event will work closely with him and be available to consult with him 24 hours a day. That person is expected to provide lodgings for Mr. Parker and/or open up their place of residence to him for the duration of the project. The latter is his preference.

"And, finally, Mr. Parker will fulfill this contract and donate all profits from the four concerts, provided his demands are met.

"Should these terms be agreeable, Mr. Parker formally accepts The Good Samaritan's Foundation proposal and will immediately begin work planning the concerts stipulated in said contract."

When I hear all of his conditions, my heart races. *That schem- ing, manipulative bastard has decided to show me how furious he is about my rejection by bringing the fight to my workplace and my home and forcing me to work with him. I have no doubt who he is going to choose as his partner for every single project. The nerve of that man! What will the directors think when he chooses me?*

I snap out of my reverie when Susan speaks up. "The board will consider your conditions, Mr. Parker. If you don't mind leav- ing us for 30 minutes or so, we would like to discuss what you've proposed. Is that acceptable?"

"That's fine, Susan. I will await your answer," Jonah said as he and his lawyer prepared to leave the room.

As soon as the door shut, Susan said, "What brought this on, I wonder? Do any of you have a problem working with him if he chooses you? I know it will be an imposition, no matter which way he decides to go. Before you consider refusing, think about what it will mean for the Foundation to have him in our corner. This could give us back most of our credibility."

There was quiet discussion as everyone voiced their worries about leaving boyfriends, spouses and children behind to work with a handsome rock star. It could mean weeks or even months of time, and losing all rights to a personal life during that time.

"Everyone, can we clear the room please? I would like to speak to Lena," Susan said, and my heart nearly stopped. *She's figured out I'm the only logical choice for this, and she's going to ask me to offer myself as the sacrificial lamb!*

Everyone all but ran from the room, shooting me apologetic looks as they went. I gave them a weak smile in return, and pre- pared to meet my fate.

Susan stared at me with a satisfied look on her face. "Lena, did you know Jonah Parker came by the office yesterday looking for you?"

"Yes, he told me."

"Did he tell you that we talked?"

"He just said you were very persuasive."

"I really wasn't. One day you'll have to tell me how you caught that man's eye. When we spoke yesterday, he was clear that you two have a professional relationship, but the look on his face told a different story. I can list a few reasons why he's been quick to re-consider our proposal, but I won't do that yet because I'd like for us to be friends when we have that conversation."

For the first time, I don't see her as my boss — I'm starting to see a potential friend. *Now that's a dangerous thought if I ever had one.* I've never really had many friends. Alex is the only exception, but then I'd trust him with my life. Something tells me Susan might fall into the same category, but I also wonder what her game is.

"I don't really know what to say."

"You don't have to say it like you just agreed to be friends with the devil. I know my position can be intimidating, but I *am* human, I promise. In fact, I predict that one day we'll be best friends.

"So, to prove my friendship I'm going to tell you something you probably don't know. Jonah Parker didn't just come up with these conditions, I guided him in that direction once I saw he might be interested in you. I didn't think you'd mind, since he's handsome, rich and famous — and he will pretty much make your career here if things go well."

My jaw nearly hit the floor. I was in shock when I realized what my scheming boss had done. *She's trying to play match-*

maker? "Why would you do that?" I asked, feeling like I'm going to pass out.

"I could see he was determined to have you, and I was just as determined to get this deal signed. However, I didn't just pimp you out to him. I made a couple of things crystal clear. I told him that whether he gave us his approval or not, your job would not be in jeopardy. I also told him that you have ultimate control over whether you agree to participate.

"You should know there are no rules against fraternization between Foundation employees and fundraisers or sponsors. So, if something were to happen between you two, the Foundation wouldn't have anything to say about it. Understand?" she asked with a pointed look.

"I understand."

"You have complete control over what you will and won't do. However, if something starts to negatively affect the project, I will step in to try to salvage it. Do you understand this as well?"

"I understand what you're implying, but it's not necessary. There is *nothing* going on between me and Jonah Parker."

"Honey, if you believe that, then you're in big trouble. This man goes full-throttle for what he wants, and I'm pretty sure he wants you. Come on, we both know he made up those conditions to guarantee he'll get to spend every minute he can with you.

"Plus, he knows you'll agree because you're passionate about this project. I think you also secretly *want* to do it because you're attracted to him too."

I am simply speechless, so she continues, "This is all yours, Lena, but if for some ridiculous reason you decide not to take this chance, I meant what I said about your job being safe. However, as your future best friend, I'm telling you that you'll regret it for the rest your life if you don't give this a chance. So, what's it going to be?"

What else can it be? This is what Gram would refer to as a sink or swim situation — and, no matter what, I always choose to swim. "Fine, I'll do it," I say, like I've just been condemned to a fate worse than death.

"Don't sound so happy about it," she said, laughing as she walked to the door to call the others back into the room. "And don't make it too easy for him."

"Oh, I won't," I told her, thinking maybe Susan and I will become friends after all.

If I'm doing this thing, the first thing I need to do is bring the fight to my turf. There are a few things he hasn't considered about all of his conditions. I can agree to them, but he can't control how I feel.

Jonah "JJ" Parker is about to get a crash course in just how much I detest being manipulated. He may think he's pulling the strings, but I'm the one in control. He cannot force me to have feelings for him — been there, done that.

I need to be careful. He clearly doesn't respect my boundaries, and has no problem using his fame and fortune to get others to do his dirty work. Well, Mr. Parker is in for the fight of his life, because I will not be used and tossed by the side of the road like trash again!

Chapter 13

"Mr. Parker, if you're agreeable, our president, Lena Walker, has agreed to be your liaison, promotion partner, and roommate for the duration of the project," Susan said, smiling.

"That's perfectly agreeable," the bastard said, wearing the smug look of someone who just won a prize at the county fair.

It's hard to believing he could be so calculating. I have to stop thinking of him like he's still my JJ. I've got to separate that person from the one who's standing in front of me today, because they're nothing alike. "Oh, I'm sure it is, Mr. Parker," I said, unable to keep the derision from my voice. "Congratulations on your win. Now, if you all will excuse me, I have to go home and prepare for a house guest — you'll be staying with me at my home. I should have everything in order by seven tonight," I said, leaving no room for argument as I made a dramatic exit from the conference room.

One hour, and quite a bit of wine later, my boiling anger has calmed to a slow simmer. *Maybe he'll hate it here, and the prob-*

lem will solve itself? Ha! Fat chance of that happening. The way my luck is going, he'll love it and want to move in permanently.

I was going to put him in the first guest room, because the one at the end of the hall is filled with boxes of things I haven't unpacked yet and I hadn't bothered to clean it. When I opened the door to get the room ready for my unwanted guest, so many memories hit me at once that I had to brace my hand on the doorframe to keep from collapsing. This had been my room growing up. There were a lot of memories floating around in this room and I didn't want to confront any of them. I hadn't even bothered with redecorating in here.

In fact, I hadn't been in here since I moved back to Atlanta. I was surprised to see my poster of JJ in all his young rock star glory was still hanging on the wall. I'd bought it with my first paycheck. I used to stare at it for hours, imagining all the adventures he was having as he toured the world. After Gram died, the only time I was happy in this room was when I was thinking about him. *Well, that poster needs to go in the trash*, I thought as I pulled it off the wall and wadded it up into a ball. T*he JJ from then is gone and he's not coming back.*

I looked at my desk, where I used to sit when I wrote to him, even after he quit writing to me. *The box!* I haven't thought about that in years. I stooped down and felt around under the bed until my fingertips brushed it.

This box, the keeper of my most treasured and most hated thoughts, needed to move somewhere else if Mr. Jonah Parker was going to be staying in this room. *It's fitting, actually, that I'm putting him in here. I avoid this room, so maybe it will help to keep me away from him when we're not working.*

I carefully took the top off the box, and tears fill my eyes. I sifted through my very own bag of bones and realized that Jonah

"JJ" Parker can never know the truth. A picture of Gram stares up at me from the bottom of the box, and it almost seems like she's disappointed in me. *Oh, Gram, you know I'm right. Don't look at me like that.*

Knowing what I had to overcome during that time, and the discipline I learned, fills me with a feeling of pride. I made my own way out, and I've become a respected businesswoman — that is until today when I nearly lost my cool because of *him.* He brings that out in me and I will never let him or anyone else ruin what I've worked so hard to achieve.

How am I going to maintain my professionalism with him living here, being with me all the time? This is not going to be easy.

I looked back down at the letter in my hand, wishing more than anything I could be anyone but me right now. *I don't know how this is supposed to work. He's already gotten under my skin in a matter of days, and I know he wants to unearth all of my secrets. I just can't let that happen. I don't need him in my life and I'm not about to let him in!*

I put the top back on the box, locking all the memories and dark secrets inside. I needed to hide it somewhere he won't think to snoop, so I went to the linen closet and buried it beneath a huge comforter on the bottom shelf. I pushed it all the way to the back, feeling confident he won't have any reason to look there. While I'm there, I grab towels, washcloths, clean sheets, a comforter, and an extra blanket and then head back to put them out for my "guest."

As I finished putting the clean sheets on and making the bed, the doorbell rang. Before I got halfway to the door, the bell rang again, and then a few seconds later it chimed a third time.

My anger from earlier resurfaced immediately. I stomped to the door and opened it with a flourish, my irritation apparent. The man standing in front of me looked nothing like the all-powerful guy who bullied me during the meeting — I saw something resembling regret and hesitancy on his face instead. *So, he isn't completely shameless. Good to know.*

"You not only invite yourself to live in my home, but you ring the doorbell like you've lost your fucking mind? Are you about done testing my patience for the day?"

Jonah sighed. "You're right, I apologize. May I please come in?"

Slightly mollified, I stepped back and motioned him to come in. He'd packed pretty light, which I hoped meant he wasn't intending to stay long. This should have made me feel better, but it didn't.

"Follow me. I set up one of the guest rooms for you. I wasn't sure how much you were bringing with you, but I think you'll have enough space for everything you've brought." I said, acting like the perfect hostess.

He doesn't seem like his usual arrogant self, but I won't ever mistake him for harmless. *Fool me once, shame on you. Fool me twice, shame on me!*

I showed him his room, and he didn't even look around. He just set his bag on the bed, and said, "Look, you're pissed at me, I get it. Can you hold off on giving me hell for a while? I know it's a lot to ask, but I don't have the energy to deal with it right now. I'm tired and I'd just like to rest."

He looked so broken, and against my better judgment I felt sorry for him. "Sure, do whatever you need to do. There are towels and washcloths in the bathroom, and there's an extra blanket in the chest at the foot of the bed. Let me know if you need anything else," I said, and then left the room as quickly as possible.

Chapter 14

I hardly slept, knowing he was under the same roof as me. *This man is going to drive me crazy!* I think as I drag myself out of bed and head to the bathroom. When I look in the mirror, a sleep-deprived, sexually frustrated, tormented version of myself is staring back at me. *Gawd, I look awful!* I have bags under my eyes, my hair looks like a fucking bird's nest, my lips look like they've never seen Chapstick a day in their life, *and* to top it off, I've got a zit. *What am I, twelve?*

It takes forever to get myself together enough to be seen without scaring people. I wonder if he's up. I want to check, but he has me feeling like an intruder in my own damn house.

Well, hiding isn't an option; I won't give him the satisfaction. I wonder, not for the first time, what he wants from me. *When he gets it, will he leave?*

Damn! The thought of him leaving scares me just as much as the thought of him staying here. This is not good. Get it through your head, you idiot — this is a temporary situation and you are not *allowed to let your emotions get out of control!*

I definitely want to hide now. I don't want to be that broken person again, always wishing, waiting, and hoping — and always disappointed. I don't want to be her again, and I won't be.

This should be a piece of cake for me. I survived the toxic waste cloud, aka Ash, for all those years — I can definitely do this.

That thought gets me moving. I throw on a pair of jeans and a t-shirt, and push my feet into my house slippers before leaving my room. As soon as I open the door, I the smell coffee and bacon. *Did he order food? It smells heavenly.*

I walk into the kitchen, and my chin damn near drops to the floor. There he is, in a fucking apron, making an omelet. He looks like he owns the damn place and, just like that, I'm mad again.

"Good morning, Lena."

"Mmm-hmm." I mutter, sounding as frigid as I feel.

"Do you like steak, egg, and cheese omelets?"

"No."

"Coffee or tea?"

"No."

"Damn, those were the only peace offerings I had," he said, obviously trying to charm me.

"Is that what this is supposed to be? Okay, fine, I'll take coffee."

"Great. Have a seat."

I feel like I've walked onto the set of some bizarre sitcom, but I need coffee before I go into battle, so I sit and wait for him to serve me.

"Thank you," I grumble stiffly before taking my first sip. I look up and realize he's staring at me and I'm immediately tense, preparing for war.

"I can see you're not going to make this easy for me, so I may as well get on with it. I know I crossed a line yesterday, but I just couldn't stop myself. I felt like the only way you'd have anything to do with me was on a professional level, so I made myself a part of your job. I thought adding the part about having to live in the same place was a stroke of genius, but I realize it's kind of intrusive now that I'm here."

So, he feels awkward, huh? I don't care. I refuse to make this easier for him. I am not some puppet he can manipulate.

"We are in a professional relationship here, so I would appreciate it if you referred to me as Ms. Walker. Only my *friends* call me Lena. You can keep your half-assed apology; I don't want it. You are not forgiven."

"Okay," he said, looking pathetic.

"I'll play the good host, and I will make sure you have clean sheets and towels, food and all of that. I will also make sure everything goes smoothly with the work, but that's it. Don't expect anything else, because you don't deserve it." I paused and took another sip of coffee to let that sink into his thick skull.

"Okay. Where do you want to start today?" he asked.

"I haven't really thought about it," I finally answered after several seconds of him staring me down and making me uncomfortable.

"Well, let me know when you get it figured out," he said.

I took that as my cue to make my getaway, so I went back to the safety of my room to get dressed for work.

Well, that was awkward. Ugh! I want to punch something right now, but I refuse to give him the satisfaction of knowing he's getting to me. He actually had the nerve to look hurt, like I kicked his puppy or something. Really? He won, and he apologizes for winning?

My head is spinning. He's acting so different and it's throwing me off my game. I've read all his media coverage, and I know no one gets one over on him. *Why is he acting like this?*

I feel like I'm in a speeding car, flying down the road out of control. My emotions are all over the place. I've got to get them locked down before they ruin me.

First, I've got to quit making everything he does so damn personal. If this was anyone else, I'd say it was business and I'd respect him for being so cunning. But he's *not* just anyone else to me. That's the whole problem.

I pick out a suit that makes me look extremely professional, and fifteen minutes later I marched back into in the kitchen to find him washing the dishes. *He's washing dishes?*

I watched as he set the sponge and plate down, and turned to face me.

"Look, I'm not a morning person and I'm not used to playing hostess. I apologize for being rude this morning. It was nice of you to make breakfast. I'm angry at you for manipulating the situation to get what you want, but I'll get past it and I *will* get the job done.

"I wake up with purpose every morning because I know the work I do matters. I refuse to let my anger at you screw that up. After all, you were one of the people who inspired me to do this kind of work in the first place."

"I inspired you?"

"You did."

"So, I'm a self-serving bastard who's also your inspiration? That's quite the contradiction. I find it funny that you're so mad at me, since you'd probably sell your soul if the damn Foundation board asked you to. Is that what this is, your attempt to schmooze me into being happy so *you* can get what *you* want? I seriously doubt you even knew anything about me before your board told you to get me on-board with their cause, so how could I inspire you to do anything?"

"I was being truthful."

"Okay then, tell me exactly what about me inspired you."

If this is what I have to do to keep the peace, I may as well do it. "I know you're a survivor. You faced unfavorable odds and you fought your way to the other side so you could come out a winner. Not only did you survive, you thrived and became a star. Your story is inspiring."

"Okay, I'll buy that."

"So, we're good?"

"Yes," he said with a devilish smile, "we're both assholes and we both like to win."

Chapter 15

After our truce, we head to the office to work out some of the logistics for the first concert. We managed to get along with each other for the entire day and actually got some things done.

"So, what kind of woman are you? Pizza Hut, Papa Johns, Dominoes, or Little Caesars?" he asks as we're wrapping up for the day.

"I like Pizza Hut Meat Lovers or their supreme."

"What the lady wants, the lady gets," he said in a chivalrous tone. "I'll worry about the food, you go ahead and leave."

I'm starving so I head home, even though I'm not a big fan of him telling me what to do. I'm trying to keep the peace, and we did accomplish some work, so I decide to be civil and not make a snarky comment.

This is starting to feel like working on any other project, instead of being punished. Now that we're on the same page, I hope we can accomplish a lot.

I intend to keep working after dinner, so when I get home I lay each of the kid's profiles out on the dining room table. They all attend different high schools, so each concert venue will be near their schools. I need to see what kind of funds we'll need to make each event special, both for the kids and to earn the Foundation some publicity. I want to be sure get the media's attention. We need to find as many ticket buyers as possible.

Jonah comes in with enough food for an army, just as I finished laying out the last packet.

"As I was driving here, I realized I eat a lot of takeout," he said, laughing as he opened each box with a flourish. "I wasn't raised that way. My mom would have dinner on the table every evening by six, and it was always homemade. She'd be tired from work, but she always cooked for us. I haven't thought about those dinners for a long time."

I have to lighten the mood, or I'm going to start feeling sorry for him again. "So, did you buy everything they had?"

"You said you like two different kinds, so I got both of those, some wings and some cheesy bread. I didn't want to forget anything."

"Well, I hope you like cold pizza for breakfast. Seriously, though, your mom sounds great."

"Both of my parents are. I was blessed when they decided to adopt me."

"What happened to your biological family, if you don't mind me asking?"

"My parents were killed in a car accident. A drunk driver crashed into them. I was five. After that, I spent two years in the system getting bounced around. If not for the Parkers, I probably would have grown up there. They were our neighbors and my parents' friends. They were on vacation when the accident happened, and by the time they got home I had already been picked up by social services. It took a while for them to find me and wade through all the paperwork. They eventually jumped through hoops, cut all the red tape, and the rest is history. You probably already knew all of that though, even though I don't really talk about it."

I didn't know what to say because I hadn't known any of that.

"Whoa! Maybe I should stop talking. That's the second time you've gone completely silent when I've shared details about my life."

Shit! Come on, Lena, don't blow it! "I'm just surprised. Now I have another reason to be inspired by you," I said, trying to think of something else to talk about.

I walked over to the cabinet to get a glass, and prepared to pour some Moscato. I clearly need it. When I turn around, I ran right into Jonah's chest, nearly dropping the glass. "Sorry," I mumbled, looking down at the floor and hoping it will swallow me. I wait a few seconds for him to move, but apparently, he has no intention of doing so. I look up and get completely lost in his beautiful eyes.

"I can't shake the feeling that I've met you before, and it only makes me want to know you more. I want to get closer and get to know the real you. It's also driving me crazy because I'm positive you're hiding something. I won't push you on it, but you need to realize that eventually everything comes to light."

He moved out of my way then, leaving me trembling. I took a deep breath, and came back at him. "That's kind of like the pot calling the kettle black, don't you think?" I asked, thinking of all of the things he's kept from the world about himself.

"There she is. I knew you wouldn't take that lying down," he said, smirking and moving closer to me again.

"Why do you like to provoke me? Don't you want to work together without fighting so we can achieve our goals?"

"I do, but I want you to give as good as you get. I want real, not what you think will keep things peaceful. Don't ever change that about yourself for me, this job, or anyone else. It's one of your best traits. You got me here, didn't you, and you did it being the authentic you."

With those words, I'm left off balance once again!

The desire I see in his eyes makes my heart skip a few beats and sends my nerves skittering. He took a step closer, looking at my face like he's trying to commit every feature to memory. When his eyes reached my lips, I watched in astonishment as he started lowering his head with the clear intention of kissing me.

When his lips touched mine, I did the only thing I *could* do — I kiss him back. Within seconds the kiss deepened, and I loved every second of it. I don't want it to stop, and apparently neither does he.

He pulled me closer, but I needed more. I let my hands skim his muscular back. Encouraged, his hands started to explore too. His mouth left mine and blazed a trail of heat down my neck. He caressed my breast, and I was lost.

This is bad! I cannot let my emotions rule my head. "We have to stop, Jonah," I said, pushing him away and trying to reign in my emotions and raw need for him.

"Why? I know you want this too."

"No, I don't. We work together. This can't happen without repercussions."

"Okay."

"Okay." *Okay? He was just filled with lust and wanting me, but now he's okay with stopping? What the hell is he playing at? It has to be some type of game. Right?*

"So, show me what you have here," he said, completely switching off the sultry look he was just wearing and motioning to the packets I've laid out on the table. And just like that, we're back to a business-only relationship.

***

The next day, Jonah surprised me by asking if I'd go somewhere with him. "Of course, that's not a problem. Where are we going?"

"You'll see. It's kind of a surprise."

"Okay, but remember we've still got a lot of work to do."

"I know, but we're not going far. Plus, we have to eat lunch at some point, so we can do two things at once."

"Okay. If you say so."

We drove for 30 minutes, and then took the exit for Berkeley Lake. "Why are we taking this exit?" I asked, confused.

"Because we're going to Berkeley Lake. There are lots of good restaurants there. My favorite is the Lazy Dog, so that's where we're going. I love their umami fries and bison burgers."

"Okay, but that really doesn't sound appealing to me. Sorry."

"That's okay. They have a huge menu, even some vegan stuff. I'm sure you'll find something you like."

"I'm feeling adventurous, so I'm game."

"Glad to hear it."

When we got there, the restaurant was pretty busy, but Jonah had reserved a table and we were seated right away. The server gave us menus and left us to decide what we'd like to order.

While we were looking at our menus, an older couple walked up, holding hands.

"Are these seats taken?" the man asked, smiling.

Jonah stood immediately and hugged each of them, then said, "Lena, these are my parents, Miranda and Phil Parker.

92

Mom, Dad, this is Lena, the president of the foundation I've been working with."

Wow, okay we're having lunch with his folks. What the hell does this mean? At least he introduced me like a colleague. It puts everything back in perspective for me. We're working together, nothing more.

"This is her, huh?" his dad asked.

"It's me," I said, smiling.

"Well, it's a relief to know our son is in such beautiful company while he's working on this project of yours, but his description of you did not do you justice. You're stunning," his mother said, embarrassing me.

"Our son has been talking nonstop about you and everything you're doing. We want to thank you for being so stubborn about making him participate in your fundraising project. You played a huge part in bringing our boy back to us."

"Yes, it's a pleasure to meet you, Lena," his dad said, hugging me. As he does, I look at Mrs. Parker over his shoulder, and she's staring at me. Her intensity is making me uneasy. *Shit! Can she see what Jonah doesn't? Does she recognize me?*

"Yes, you certainly are beautiful…" his mother said slowly.

"Well, thank you so much," I said, feeling like I'm on the hot seat.

"You're very welcome. Did Jonah ever tell you what I did before I retired?" she asked as we take our seats at the table.

"No, I don't believe so."

"I was a forensic anthropologist. I worked with bones and reconstructing ancient skeletons. In fact, I was the head of my department before I retired last year. When I see people, I'm always interested in their bone structure. Everyone is different, and it's sort of like a fingerprint to me. Once I've studied your bones, I'll never forget your face."

She knows who I am! Shit, that means she'll tell him. "That's amazing. You must miss your job."

"Yes, I do. There are some times when I miss it more than others. ... I'd love to have you two over for dinner soon. I know it can't be right away because you still have some busy weeks coming up. I also imagine you have a lot of things to...figure out."

"Yes, we do," I said, understanding perfectly what she's not saying.

"Good. We'll get together soon then. You should know, I'm quite stubborn too, so don't think you're getting out it."

Fuck! This double meaning-filled conversation is about to make my head explode. "Yes, ma'am."

The rest of the meal seemed to be pleasant for everyone but me. They were talking and laughing and acting totally normal, while I was having a complete nervous breakdown in my head. Most of my inner monologue was punctuated by *Shit!* and my thoughts were circling the horrible fact that I was going to have to admit who I was. *I don't think, in my heart of hearts, I'd ever planned to tell him. Shit! Why did this have to happen just when things seemed to be going well?*

After what seemed like an eternity, the meal was finally over and we were all getting ready to leave. I was smiling and doing an Academy Award-winning performance, but I really wanted to get out of there.

"Lena, dear, it was such a pleasure to meet you," Jonah's mother said, patting my arm. "I'm so glad Jonah finally agreed to introduce us."

"Me, too, Mrs. Parker. It was great to meet you both," I said, smiling for all I'm worth.

"Now, don't forget about that dinner invitation — because I won't," she said in a mildly threatening way.

"Oh, I can guarantee I won't," I said, laughing in a way that sounds a little hysterical to my ears.

"Great. When you find a good date, have Jonah let us know."

"It was good meeting you, Lena," Jonah's dad said, giving me a brief hug. "I hope we'll be seeing more of you soon."

We parted ways and headed to our cars. As we got ready to get in, I heard his father say, "I like her," which was nice, but I could feel his mother's stare burning holes into my back from across the parking lot. *I am in deep shit!*

***

We've managed to work together without incident for the last three weeks. We've accomplished a lot, too. The candidates are receiving the medical care they need, all paid for by Jonah's first concert. He even met with each of them individually and gave them a pep talk.

He told them how he felt about his transplant, and how he conquered his fear and recovered. He also let them know they had more to accomplish and they needed to live in order to do it. It was amazing to hear. Listening to him talk to them was like listening to the JJ I fell for all of those years ago.

The Board members were extremely happy with how the first concert went, and they'd started calling us the "dynamic duo." They were also thrilled that everything for the second concert was on schedule and ready to go.

The proceeds from this concert were earmarked to pay for the kids' rehab needs. Jonah even ended up going shopping for each family to guarantee the kids all had the nutritious foods they needed waiting for them when they finally got to go home.

I was having fun getting things done, and I was enjoying my time with Jonah. When I realized this, I was scared shitless! It was getting harder and harder to dislike him, and that was a dangerous thing for me.

I was a little nervous about the upcoming concert, there were a lot of details to handle. I normally wasn't so involved with all the bits and pieces that went into projects like this, but Jonah's conditions meant I had to deal with all of them. I realized I was okay with that though, and really enjoyed all the work.

I even went with Jonah when he rehearsed. Every time I heard him sing, I got the same feeling of awe I had that day all those years ago at the hospital.

Everything was going well, but there was still an underlying sexual tension haunting everything Jonah and I did together. The only thing that was truly bothering me about our arrangement was where Jonah went when he mysteriously vanished at the same time every day. It was driving me crazy that he wouldn't tell me what he was doing.

I knew I should just let it go. I didn't need to know what he was doing every second of every day. I think we were kind of becoming friends though, so it really bothered me that he didn't trust me enough to tell me where he was going.

Of course, my mind takes me to all kinds of crazy places. Does he have a gambling habit? Is he seeing someone? I can't figure it out. It's stupid for me to begrudge him his secret, when I'm the queen of secrets, but it doesn't change how I feel.

Sometimes the urge to tell him everything and unburden myself is so fucking overwhelming. What keeps me from telling him everything is, I don't want to risk losing him all over again. I just can't do it. So, I let him keep his little secret so I can keep my big one.

Chapter 16

Some days, the memories really fuck with my mind. Today is one of those days. It's close to nine at night, and we're in Jonah's rental car, leaving one of the suggested venues for the final concert.

"A beautiful night, in a beautiful city, with a beautiful woman," Jonah said, rocketing me back to the past. I'm lost there, in my memories, practically drowning.

"Lena?" Jonah called, tapping my shoulder lightly.

"Yes, I'm listening."

"Bullshit. Where'd you go just now?"

"To the past."

"Was it a good memory?" he asked, and I smile because it was — bittersweet, but good.

"Do you want to share?"

"Uh no, that's not happening."

"Of course, not," he said, hostility lacing his voice. "You never do."

"Excuse me?"

"You heard what I said, Lena. You never share anything about yourself."

"Don't do this, Jonah. It was a great day, please don't ruin it."

"Wow. I just thought we were—"

"You thought we were what, Jonah?"

"Wow, thanks for that. Good to see some things don't change."

"Are you seriously getting offended because I don't want to share my private thoughts with you? You don't trust me enough to tell me where you sneak off to each day, so why should I trust you?" *There I said it.*

"If you wanted to know, all you had to do was ask. It's no damn secret."

"Really? Why didn't you just tell me then?"

"Oh, like you volunteer everything about *your* private life?"

"I keep my private life to myself. It's my choice who I tell what. That's why I didn't demand that you tell me what you're doing. Your private life is yours and you can decide who you tell about it."

"I go to visit my parents," he said after a few tense seconds.

"I don't want to hear your lies, and I don't really need to know what you're doing. I was just making a point."

"Lies? When have I ever lied to you about anything?"

"Maybe not lie, but you do scheme and manipulate to get what you want. You can't deny that."

"I thought we were past that."

"You asked. I simply answered."

"Lena, I am not lying to you. I really have been going to see my parents. Haven't you noticed that I never mention anything about them? You never see me with them in the tabloids, and when you look at my biography they aren't even mentioned."

Of course, none of this has escaped my attention, I just never knew why.

When I didn't comment, he continued, "Look, something happened to me after I came out of that surgery. The road to recovery was hell, and I struggled daily to not resent the fact that I survived and that *she* made me want to survive."

"I assume you are talking about Sky? The girl you called your angel?"

"Yes, her."

"Why would you resent her?"

"Because she made me want to live. I was fine with my diagnosis, until I met her. She was there for a while, being my cheerleader and sounding board, but then she just disappeared from my life without even saying goodbye. I know, that without her I wouldn't have made it off that table. She was important to me and then she was just gone."

"As time went by, I began to resent her and everyone else, especially my parents. I pushed them away, put everything into my singing career, and I never looked back. By the time I realized what I was doing, I'd put so much distance between us that I was scared I'd lost them.

"I wanted to rebuild our relationship, so I paid them back for all of my medical bills, paid off their home, and hired some help to take care of things around the house for them. I made sure they never have to work again if they don't want to. I wanted to give them what they'd lost trying to keep me alive. I just wanted my parents back and I wanted their lives to be as easy as possible so they could do all the things they never had the money to do before because of me."

"That's nice. I never would have suspected."

"I miss them, and I need them in my life. I'm tired of just existing in this life they fought so hard to let me live. All the money, cars and things I possess are nothing if I have no family to share them with. I want to start feeling again. Well, I thought I did, until a saucy little minx came into my life, and now I feel *too much*," he said as we pulled into my driveway.

"Um, thanks for telling me. Starting tomorrow we have a long week ahead of us, and we need to rest up. I'm going to call it a night," I said, quickly getting out of the car and making my way to the door like the devil himself was on my heels. I went straight to my bedroom, shut the door and stayed there the rest of the night. I couldn't deal with his revelations and I didn't want to be tempted to open up to him.

The next day was hectic, and I got to feel what it's like to be an actual celebrity, firsthand. The fans, the limos, the photo shoots, the questions from fans coming from every direction... it was over-whelming and I wondered how Jonah dealt with it. I'm surprised no one in the media has figured out where he's staying. According to Jonah, that still might happen because, in his words, the vultures are persistent. *I'm just thankful this is not my everyday life!*

We go our separate ways as the final details are all ironed out. He has to get warmed up and I have to make sure the show will run without a hitch.

In no time, it's show time. The venue is filled to capacity and there's an excited buzz going through the audience. The feeling of déjà vu is overwhelming, even though I'm standing in the wings this time instead of being out there in the crowd.

"It's crazy, right?" Jonah asked, walking up beside me.

"What?"

"The fans, the anticipation, everything," he said as someone from the auxiliary staff walked up and handed him a mic. "It's show time, Angel," he said, and walked onto the stage, leaving me speechless and scared.

Angel? That's what he used to call me. Have I slipped up? Has he figured it out? I'd know, right? Shit!

"Well, if it isn't Ms. Fancypants President," I heard coming from behind me, saving me from going into full-on panic mode.

I absolutely lose it. "Oh my God, Alex!" I scream, jumping into his arms. He spins me around, and hugs me tight. I can't believe he's here. He set me back on my feet and I just looked at him. "What are you doing here?"

"I got a call from a Ms. McKinley telling me that my best friend is putting on another concert and I needed to be here. She also roped me into participating in your silly bachelor auction. You do remember your promise to me, right?" he asked innocently.

"Of course! I would have called you, but Jo—" I stopped unsure of where I was about to go with that statement. Did I really not call or even consider Alex as my date for the auction because I was holding out hope that Jonah would ask me? I already knew the answer to that — yes. *When the hell did this happen? We are not a couple. This is not a romance. What the hell am I thinking?*

"Lena?" Alex prompted, since I've gone off to la-la land.

"No, of course I haven't forgotten. I just figured you were busy. I haven't really had a moment to catch my breath. This contract with Jonah is taking up all my time."

"Every moment, of every hour?" he asked, looking at me with an expression I do not like at all.

"It's not like that Alex. Stop it. You know me," I said, grabbing his hand and squeezing it.

"You're right, I do know you. I know *him*, too."

"Look, we'll talk about this later. For now, I just want to enjoy the fact that you're here in Atlanta!" I said, embracing him again. I didn't realize how much I'd missed him until he was standing right there. He's been my lifeline for as long as I've known him.

"I literally just came from the airport, and I'm exhausted."

"Shit, of course you are. I'll text you my address, and here are the keys to my house. I haven't cleaned the other guest room — Jonah's staying in the one I had set up — so just take my room for tonight. I can sleep on the couch and I'll get the room set up for you tomorrow," I said, as I text him my address and alarm code.

"Wait, he's *living* with you?"

"I know, I know. I'll explain after you've had some rest. It's not what you think, so get your mind out of the gutter."

"Okay, but tomorrow, we're going to talk," he said before walking away.

Shit, well my weekend just got a little bit more interesting. All three of us in one house...

The concert lasted two hours, and on the final song, Jonah walked over into the wings, grabbed my hand, and dragged me out onto the stage, taking me completely by surprise.

"This woman here is a hero," he said to the audience. "She's the president of the Foundation responsible for making this concert and everything we've done for these kids possible. I want to thank her for letting me be a part of making their dreams come true, and for being so persistent. Let's give a huge thank you to the lovely Ms. Lena Walker!" he shouted, grabbing my hand and raising it.

To my astonishment, the crowd cheered for me! It was such a high, and Jonah was the one who gave me this moment. I looked over at him smiling at me, and nothing and no one else exists. Then he pulled me close and kissed me. The crowd continued to cheer as we walk off the stage.

"You didn't have to do that."

"I wanted to. It's probably the first time I've done exactly what I wanted during the whole time we've worked on this project."

Chapter 17

I pulled into my driveway forty-five minutes later, and gave in to fatigue. Who knew how much work would be involved in putting on so many concerts in such a short time? I'm also worried about Jonah's comment about not getting what he wanted, but it's too much to think about tonight.

I unlocked the door, set my purse down on the dining room table and walked into my bedroom, thinking about nothing but falling into bed and sleeping so I could get away from the stress and worry that's followed me around since this whole ordeal began.

I hear a noise in the hall and immediately think, *Shit! I completely forgot about Alex being here.* I make my way down toward Jonah's room and there's Alex, sitting on the floor in the hallway with the contents of *the* box spread out around him. He looked up at me like he doesn't know me.

"I didn't want to kick you out of your own bed, considering my unscheduled drop-in, so I was going to take the couch. I came looking for a comforter, and I found one. I also found this box. I would've put it back, but the lid came off and there was a photograph on top. I've never seen any childhood pictures of you and I was curious. But, *this?* What the hell is this, Lena?" he asked, looking up at me accusingly.

"Alex, let's not do this right now. Just forget it."

"Forget it? Fuck, no! Is this an obsession? Why have you been following Jonah's career like a stalker all these years? Is that why you're friends with me, so you could get to him? Also, when the hell did you have a baby, and who the hell is JJ?"

"Alex, just let me—"

"Let you what, Lena? Explain? How the fuck can you explain all of this? Does Parker know about this crazy obsession of yours?"

"Of course, he doesn't. Do you think he'd be here if he did?"

"I don't know what to think. I'm just finding out that my best friend is not the kind of woman I thought she was. You knew I was friends with Jonah. Did you use me to get to him? Was this your plan all along?"

He sounded hurt, and I understand why he thinks that. "No, Alex. Meeting you was completely unplanned, you know that. Please, we have to clean this up. Once we're done, I'll explain everything. Okay?"

"I don't know, maybe I should just go."

"No! Please don't go. You're my best friend. Just give me a chance to explain. Please! You *know* me. Please, Alex?"

"Fine."

We quickly put the comforter back in the closet, and I grabbed the box before heading to my bedroom. After that, Alex and I sat down, and I talked for an hour. I told him everything — even Jonah's mom's reaction, and what she said to me.

"Wow. That's one hell of a story. You're right— you *are* in deep shit. Do you think she's going to tell him?"

"I think she's giving me time to do it myself. I just don't know how much."

"What are you going to do? Are you going to tell him everything or just the part his mom knows? I mean, there's a child involved."

"Even if I told him about that, there is literally nothing he could do about it. The baby was adopted. She has a better life than I could've given her and she's happy and healthy."

"Thank you for telling me the truth. Now that I know everything, I understand why you did what you did. Just remember, you always have me in your corner. You know that, right?"

"Of course, I do. You're my best friend."

"You know I want to be more than that, and I could be if you'd just let me. Ash isn't in the picture anymore, and you're not with Jonah. So, what's stopping you?"

"Alex, I—"

"I'm sorry. This is not the time or the place. You have other things going on. All I ask is that you consider it. We're good as friends, but we could be better as a couple," he said and kissed me on the cheek.

"I'll think about it."

"Good. It's been a long night. Get some rest," he said as he put the top back on the box and handed it to me. He planted another kiss on the top of my head and left the room. I closed my eyes and flopped back on the bed. *My life has gone from complicated to nearly impossible in just a few hours.*

Chapter 18

Alex closed the door to Lena's bedroom as quietly as he could. He was deep in thought and his head was spinning with the information he'd just learned. *Jonah asked me to help him find a woman named Sky, and I did. I didn't understand why then, but I do now. Hell, I think I was friend-zoned with Lena from the start. Shit, now I know exactly who Sky is and where to find her, but I can't tell Jonah!*

As he walked down the hall, still mulling this latest development, he came face to face with a surprised Jonah. They stared at each other, and Alex felt the familiar resentment rear its ugly head. *I haven't felt that jealousy in years,* Alex thought, *and I really don't want to go back to feeling that way, but I also don't want to lose out to him again. I can't believe how things have turned out.*

"Long time no speak, Jo," Alex said once he recovered from the shock of seeing his friend standing there.

"I could say the same."

"I had every intention of calling you to catch up, but here you are."

"No kidding?" Jonah asked with a hint of sarcasm. "Okay. So, how do you know Lena and why are you coming out of her bedroom in the middle of the night?"

"It's an interesting story. I'm guessing it's just about as interesting as the story of how you came to be living here with her."

"I imagine it is."

"I've talked about my best friend a bunch of times," Alex said by way of explanation. "Remember, I told you I hired her away from her asshole ex-boyfriend, the one who'd been my agent. That was back when she lived in Seattle."

"Wait, Lena is your best friend?"

"One and the same."

"That's crazy. I had no idea. That explains a lot."

"Yeah, it does. Your turn."

"I remember you talking about her and I got the clear impression you wanted more than a friendship."

"What if I did?"

"Do you?"

Alex laughed, but didn't answer. "Have a goodnight, Jo. I'll see you in the morning."

"You're staying here too?"

"Yeah, I'm here for the weekend. Goodnight," Alex said as he walked in the direction of the dusty guest room.

Chapter 19

"**S**weetie, it's time to wake up," Alex said, and I opened my eyes to see him sitting on the edge of my bed. *I forgot he's a morning person. Ugh!* I looked behind him and saw Jonah standing in the doorway, and he looked pissed. *My life has become a little too interesting lately!*

"It's ten o'clock, and we have to be at the auction venue to meet the event planner in an hour," Jonah said impatiently. "I have to be back here by two for a photo shoot, plus I need to get a tuxedo for the auction tonight. Rise and shine, *sweetie*," Jonah said, mocking Alex as he turned to leave.

"What do you have planned today, besides getting bid on by a bunch of horny Atlanta women?" I asked Alex.

"Just a little shopping."

"Well, I've got my marching orders from Mr. Cheerful there, so I guess I'll see you at the auction. It's time for me to get moving," I said as I got up and headed to the bathroom.

Forty-five minutes later, Jonah and I were driving to the auction venue to meet the event planner. There were some last-minute details to be dealt with so the auction could run smoothly.

God, I haven't even had a chance to think about what Alex said last night, Lena thought during the uncomfortable silence in the car. *I kind of knew he had romantic feelings for me, but I could ignore what I suspected because he never said anything. Now that he's put it out there, I'm going to have to be careful that I don't lose him as my friend. I don't want to hurt him, but I also don't feel that way about him.*

"So, when the hell were you going to tell me that you were best friends with Alexander Malone?" Jonah practically shouted, interrupting my thoughts. "Hell, you didn't even tell me he was going to be staying at your house. I had to bump into him when he was coming out of your bedroom last night."

"There you go acting entitled again. Who the fuck do you think you are? First of all, let's get something straight. *You* are a guest in *my* home. I *do not* have to clear my other house guests with you. Alex is my best friend and he has a standing invitation."

"I'm the man who kissed you in front of a crowd of people last night. That's who the fuck I am."

The minute I put the car in park, he hopped out, slamming the door. I'm was left staring at him, wondering what the heck just happened.

When I finally walked into the building, he was sitting down with the planner acting like things were business as usual. About halfway through the meeting, he got a call and excused himself.

When he left the room, I felt like I could breathe for the first time since we left the house. Even the planner could tell something was wrong. I think she wanted the meeting to be over almost as much as I did.

An hour later, we'd finally ironed out all the details and the meeting ended, and we made the drive back in complete silence.

The minute I stopped the car, Jonah was out and walking straight for his rental car. I had no idea where he was going.

I'd really hoped we could have a civil conversation before Alex got back because I could only handle so much testosterone at one time. I watched as Jonah pulled out of the driveway, squealing his tires as he made the turn. *Well, guess he's madder than I thought.*

I didn't really have much time to worry about Jonah's temper tantrum. I had a fancy bachelor auction to get ready for, and it was already late morning. I didn't want to be alone, so I decided to do something completely out of my comfort zone — call Susan.

"Hey, have you already done your shopping for the auction?" I asked when she answered her cell.

"No. Want to go shopping?" asked excitedly.

"Yes! Cumberland, Stonecrest, or Lenox?"

"We're not *going* shopping, I have just the dress for you. Come over, I'm home. My address is 770 Piedmont Ave."

"Um, okay," I said, though what she said was kind of weird. "I'm on my way. We can still go get beautified, right? I need the works!"

"Honey, leave it to me!"

"Be there in fifteen." I said, hanging up. I guess having a girlfriend does have advantages.

Susan lived in a beautiful condominium in the Buckhead area. When I knocked, she opened the door for me, looking totally put together as always.

"Hey, girl! I can't wait until you see what I've got in my closet. You'll just die! Come on in my bedroom and have a seat."

She disappeared into a huge closet, and asked, "What colors do you like? I have them all."

"I was thinking green."

"Perfect! It goes with your skin tone. I have one that will look fabulous on you," she said as she came out of the closet holding an emerald green dress.

"It's absolutely stunning," I said as I looked at the low-cut satin gown. "This is definitely *the* dress! How did you know just what I'd like?"

"Well, I wanted to be a stylist when I was younger, and eventually I expanded to design. It's just me, so when I'm not working at the Foundation, I design things to fill my closet."

"You made this?"

"Yep. It's an original McKinley."

"Oh, my God. I can't believe I didn't know this!" I exclaimed, looking at all the other dresses hanging in her enormous closet.

"Well, now that we're friends, we can tell each other stuff like this. Right?" she asked, looking hopeful.

"Sure. Just realize that I don't get close to people easily. I've been hurt pretty badly in the past, so I'm careful about letting people in," I said, trying to make her understand.

"I get it. But, there are advantages to having *female* best friends. Like gossiping about that beautiful man you're friend-zoning. You know, the one who worships the ground you walk on."

Damn, is it that obvious? "Okay, fine. Besties?" I ask, extending my hand to shake. She swatted my hand away and pulled me in for a hug.

"From now on, I'm Sue to you. All of my friends call me Sue. I know I'm your boss, but I consider us equals. There would be no Foundation left if you hadn't come along.

"Okay, enough serious talk. Let's open some champagne and we can gossip about your love life while you try on the dress to make sure I don't need to alter it. Once that's done, we'll go get beautified."

The crazy thing was, for the first time, I needed to talk to about all of the shit going on in my life. Normally, I'd talk to Alex, but since he's part of what's going on, that option was out. I wanted an honest opinion about what I should do, so I'd have to come clean — about everything. *Can I really trust someone with all my secrets? I don't want to be this unapproachable woman. I want to have a life and friends and, eventually, a real relationship. In the past, I always chose to be closed off so I could protect myself. That ends today.*

Sue came back carrying two glasses and a bottle of champagne. "Okay, drink up. Our appointment at *A Woman's Paradise Spa* is at 2:30. I booked us for the full package: massage, nails, full body wax, hair, and makeup. We'll be the best-looking bitches at that damn auction. Now, spill. I want all the juicy details."

I told her everything, every damn thing. She all but ate popcorn as she listened to me. When I was finished, she was quiet, and it made me super nervous. "Okay, what are you thinking?"

"I'm speechless. This is like some kind of big screen shit. What the hell are you going to do?"

"I have no idea."

"So, you've never had anything romantic with Alexander?"

"Correct."

"Do you want to?"

"Honestly, I don't really see it happening. I don't want to tell him though, because I'm terrified I'll lose him as a friend."

"I understand," she said, and looked a little sad.

"Really? What do you think I should do?"

"Both of those men are seriously attracted to you. I already knew about Jonah, hell I encouraged him to go after you. But I had no idea about Alexander," she said, getting that same forlorn look on her face..

"Why do you look like I just broke your favorite doll?"

"It's nothing. I just hoped that…" she stopped, and looked away from me.

I nudged her with my elbow. "Hoped what? C'mon, we're best friends now. Remember?" I said, earning a smile from her.

"When I reached out to Mr. Malone, I was kind of hoping to meet him. I've always had a thing for him."

"Oh, shit. You like Alex?"

"A little. … Okay, maybe a lot."

"Is that why you called him and asked him to come this weekend?"

"Yes, partly. I also thought you might need a friend, since you weren't warming up to my offer. So, I took a chance and called him."

I said nothing because the wheels in my head were too busy turning.

"I'm sorry. I know I was probably sticking my nose where it didn't belong—"

"Sue, do you want to see if there's something there with Alex?" I asked, cutting her off.

"Alex?"

"Sorry, I call him Alex. I meant Alexander. Do you want a chance to see if sparks fly between you?"

"Of course, I do. But he—"

"But nothing. Come on, let's go. We are *not* missing that spa appointment. We have shit to do."

The men don't stand a chance, because I have a plan. I'm not good at manipulation, but I'm about to master it, and flip the switch on Mr. Jonah Parker.

On the drive to the spa, Sue's mind was whirling. *I'm exhausted just thinking about the amount of pressure Lena's under. I can't believe she's been keeping all those secrets. Guess that's another thing we have in common. After she faced her fears and came clean to me, I want to do the same thing. I just hope she won't hate me when I tell her.*

"Lena. I have something to confess."

"Can it wait? I'm ready to relax and let my brain shut off for a while."

"No, it can't wait, because I don't know if you'll want to be around me after I tell you."

"Okay. I'm not going anywhere — we're flying down the highway doing eighty. Hit me with it."

"I know I told you we didn't hire you because of Alexander's referral, but it did play a huge part in why I was your main cheer-leader. It was clear from his letter of recommendation that he cared about you, but I thought I might be able to get close to him and make him interested in me. It's awful, I know.

"I had no idea you had connections to Jonah, but when I saw he was interested in you, I gave him a pretty big push in your direction to keep him around so you'd be romantically occupied.

"Here's the really bad part. I asked Alexander to come here because I wanted him to see you with Jonah and realize he didn't have a chance with you. I hoped with you out of the picture, he'd see me as something more than your boss.

"But I really want you as my friend, and I feel guilty about what I did. Can forgive me?"

"Okay," Lena says, smiling at her new friend. "The truth is, I owe *you*, Sue. You set a lot of wheels in motion and made things happen that might never have happened otherwise. I want Jonah — I've always wanted him. When you gave him that push, you also forced me to acknowledge my feelings, even though I've been fighting it, and him the whole time. It doesn't matter how it all started, or why you did it. I should be thanking you."

Chapter 20

Four primped and pampered hours later, the two women were made up and dressed to kill. They'd also come up with a perfect plan to get what they both wanted. When they got to the site of the auction, they told the Board members and staff that there had been a slight change of plan and the auction would now have a twist. Soon, everyone was convinced it would be fun and spontaneous, and they were on-board with the idea.

Of course, there were only two couples who would be experiencing the twist, but no one but Lena and Sue knew that.

The auction was going smoothly and everyone was having a great time as the female auctioneer announced, "Next up is eligible bachelor number five, Alexander Malone. Alexander is a talented thirty-three-year-old actor and popular television host for ET. He's single, has no kids, and is one gorgeous work of manly art. Ladies let's start the bidding at eight thousand."

"Eight thousand!" someone in the crowd shouted.

"Eight thousand, do I have nine?" the auctioneer asked. Radio silence. Not one woman raised her hand.

"Nine thousand!" Lena shouted. Alex smiled sheepishly at the bid.

"Anyone else? … Going once, going twice … Sold! One night with Alexander Malone for the lovely goddess in green! Step right up and claim your prize!" the auctioneer said with enthusiasm.

That was my cue. I got up, and made my way up to claim him. We were then escorted off stage, where we joined the other bidders and their men.

"Next up is bachelor number six, Jonah Parker! Jonah is an award-winning recording artist. He's single, and he's ready to mingle. Ladies, let's start the bidding at fifteen thousand!"

Not one woman raised her hand with a bid. Jonah's look of confusion was the absolute highlight of my night. I squirmed as Jonah's eyes found mine in the crowd. *This is going to be so good.*

"Fifteen thousand dollars, right here!" Sue yelled.

"Fifteen thousand dollars for one night with the talented Jonah Parker. Do I hear twenty?" the auctioneer asked hopefully. When no one responded, she said, "Sold to the beauty in silver! Step right up, and claim your man!"

The auction continued, but I quit paying attention. I watched as Sue and Jonah began walking in our direction. Suddenly it felt like my dress was cutting off my circulation, and I couldn't breathe. *Oh God! I literally have two seconds to get my shit together before they'll be standing in front of me.*

"Ms. Walker! You look stunning this evening," Sue said, smiling from ear to ear as they came to a stop in front of Alex and me.

"Thank you. You look quite ravishing too, Ms. McKinley."

"Do we need to leave you two alone?" Jonah asked stoically.

"Of course not, I apologize for being so rude. Sue, I don't believe you've formally met my best friend Alexander "Alex" Malone. Alex, this is Sue McKinley, my boss."

As I turned to look at Alex, I noticed he was looking at Sue in the weirdest way.

I poked my elbow into his side, and he jumped before saying, "Oh, sorry. It's nice to meet you in person, Ms. McKinley. You're the reason I'm here."

"I am, yes."

"Well, it seems I'm in your debt."

"Not at all, it was my pleasure," she said, flashing him a devastating smile.

Sheesh! Poor Alex, Lena thought. *He doesn't know it yet, but with the way he's looking at her, I think Sue will definitely be able to work her magic. I've never seen Alex react like that.*

The voice of the evening's MC cut through the chatter, and we heard, *"Ladies, we need the winning bidders to make a single file line at the registration table. You'll need to give us your name, your winning bid amount, and your bachelor's number.*

"When you're done with that, please step to your right and make your payment. When you've paid, you'll receive a number. Please walk out the double doors and go to the limousine bearing that number. Your bachelor will be waiting for you there!"

"Bachelors! The limo drivers will be holding signs with your name and number on them. Find your driver and give them your itinerary for the night, then get comfortable and enjoy some refreshments while you wait for your lady to join you.

"Enjoy your night and thank you for participating in the Good Samaritan's Foundation Auction."

"Well, I guess we'll see you guys soon," I said to Alex and Jonah, as Sue and I started toward the registration table.

"See you soon," Jonah said to Sue.

"I'll be waiting," Alex said to me, squeezing my hand.

We watched as they walked out the double doors, and I turned and smile at Sue. "Are you ready for this?"

"What choice do I have now, it's done. Let's go get our numbers, so it looks like we're playing along."

We walked through the double doors a little while later, and looked at the line of limos. I squeezed Sue's hand. "Good luck. I hope this night is everything you want it to be. Let's meet up for drinks and dish tomorrow. Deal?" *I feel like such a mastermind! I can't believe we're doing this.*

"Deal. See you tomorrow," Lena said before walking to her assigned limo.

"Good evening, miss. My name is Carlos and I will be your chauffeur tonight," the driver said as I approached. "Your bachelor awaits." He opened the door and I slid easily into the seat and turned to face the man I most likely hurt my best friend's feelings to be with.

"Aren't you in the wrong car?" Jonah asked, as I got settled in the comfy leather seat.

"Nope. I am exactly where I should be. Didn't I mention the name for this event was Auction With a Twist? The men we bid on tonight are not the ones who get to take us on a date."

"Wow. I'm surprised you're happy about this turn of events. I didn't think you were capable of living without your precious *Alex*," he said bitterly.

"Are you disappointed that I'm your date?" I asked, trying to stop fidgeting as his eyes traveled from my face to my lips, down to my cleavage and then all the way to the slit in my dress where my fabulously waxed legs were on display.

"No, I'm not disappointed. Are you?" he asked, reaching over to the built-in bar and pouring a glass of wine.

"No, I'm not disappointed at all. What do you have planned for us tonight?"

"Just a simple dinner at a private venue."

"Wow, fancy. You really know how to wow a girl."

"If you say so."

"I absolutely do not, that was sarcasm. Well, let's get to your *private venue* then."

"No, I don't think so. You wanted a twist, right?"

"If we're not going to dinner, then where are we going?"

"To your house."

"What? Are you serious? I spent hours getting ready for this night out—"

"I want to take you there and do all the things I've been dreaming about doing to you since the day we met."

"Oh."

"Oh, as in okay?"

Am I in? I've wanted to be with him again for more than ten years! Okay, I have to play this cool. "I'm in," I said quietly.

"Well then, our night is about to start," he said as he took out his phone and hit a speed dial number. "Philippe? This is Mr. Parker. I'm afraid I have to cancel my reservation. I apologize for the inconvenience and I'll be sending you and your staff generous compensation for your trouble. ... Thank you for understanding," he said ending the call and knocking on the limo's partition. Almost immediately our chauffeur lowered it to get his instructions.

"Change of plans, Carlos. We're going to Ms. Walker's home," he said and gave him the address.

"Yes, sir," Carlos said, typing the address into his GPS.

After the partition was back up, Jonah poured another glass of wine and handed it to me, then said, "I'd like to make a toast."

"A toast? What are we toasting?"

"To making it count," he said, clinking his glass with mine and smiling.

The fifteen minutes it took to get to my house were the absolute longest fifteen minutes of my life! By the time we pulled into the driveway, I had already fantasized about three different scenarios, all of which involved jumping Mr. Jonah Parker and giving him the night of his life.

When we finally got there, Carlos opened the doors and we got out. "We'll be staying here for the remainder of the evening," Jonah said, dismissing Carlos.

"Shall we?" Jonah asked, as Carlos got into the limo to leave.

"Yes, I think it's about time we did."

Chapter 21

Jonah hurried me into the house and then closed and locked the door behind us. When he turned around, I could see how much he wanted me and, this time, I was going to make sure he got me.

I took his hands and pulled him toward me, staring straight into his eyes as I did it. I wanted him so badly at this point, I was ready to tear his clothes off and have him right there in the entryway.

He kissed me slowly and stopped my hands from exploring him. He started with kissing me on the mouth, then trailed kisses down my neck, all the while keeping me from touching him. It was maddening and *so* hot.

As if by magic, my dress was suddenly pooled around my ankles and I was standing there in just my lacy black thong and my stilettos. He stepped back and looked me up and down, smiling like the Cheshire cat.

"Ms. President, I do believe you've lost your dress, but I think I prefer you this way," he said, then pulled me close and kissed me hard.

I melted into him, relishing the warm embrace I'd waited so long to feel again. I dragged my fingernails through his hair and rubbed my clit on the huge bulge in his pants.

He wanted me so badly he was shaking. He devoured my lips like the starving man he was. The uncertainty was gone, and neither of us would be denied tonight.

I was so fucking turned on by his need and I was ready to take charge and speed up the pace. I pulled my mouth from his and drew a line down his neck with my tongue, nibbling my way southward, undoing his dress shirt as I went.

My lips traced his ridiculously defined abs all the way down to the ultimate prize. I knew what I wanted from him and I knew exactly how to get it. How many times had I daydreamed about this over the years? Okay, *I need to slow this down. I've waited too long to let this be over in a few minutes of frantic fucking.*

I slowly unfastened his pants and let them fall around his ankles, mimicking my dress. He stepped out of them and just stood there, waiting for me to remove the last barrier between us. I traced a delicate trail over the pulsating bulge beneath the cloth, and earned a low moan for my efforts.

I pulled down his Emporio boxers and let them join his pants on the floor, releasing his imprisoned dick. I took in the sight of his manhood standing proud and throbbing, then looked up into his eyes. *This is just like I've pictured it so many times.*

I bent my head and dragged the tip of my tongue up his length, and kissed the drops of pre-cum gathered at the tip. With another sultry glance up at him, I took his dick into my mouth and began aggressive, long slippery strokes.

The hell with slowing down! I want him, and he wants this. I sucked harder, taking his entire length, and rocking my head against his tensed muscles. I felt him shudder, and then shudder again. The head of his dick swelled in my mouth, signaling his approaching climax.

A stifled growl left his lips as he rammed himself forward and quivered in pure ecstasy. Another cry filled the room as he gave in to my motions and filled my throat. I swallowed all of it and released him, smiling up at him in triumph. I'd waited a long time for that.

Jonah panted, leaning against the door. Finally, he opened his eyes and looked at me. "Guess it's my turn to return the favor," he said with a devilish smile.

Jonah kissed me passionately, as we started moving in the direction of the bedroom. When they got to the foot of the bed, he pushed me back until I dropped onto the bed. He went after my black thong with his teeth and dragged it down to expose my wet pussy. With that obstacle out of the way, he spread my legs and buried his face right where I wanted him.

His efforts were rewarded almost instantly, as a massive orgasm rocked me. This made Jonah's cock stiffen again, and in an instant, Lena was beneath him, mesmerized by the heat of the moment, her full breasts filling his gaze. He ground is face into them, biting. She yelped in pleasured pain as her nipples stiffened. His dick slid effortlessly into her, and he hammered it home. She grabbed hold of his ass, pulling him deeper. She kissed him, tasting her orgasm on his tongue.

He showed no signs of stopping as wave after wave of ecstasy shook her. She gasped for air, as pleasure and pain warred for dominance and her second orgasm hit like a tsunami.

When her body finally stopped shaking, she smiled at him lazily, as she happily floated in a haze of sexual satisfaction. Instead of smiling back, he reached down and flipped her onto her stomach, then circled her waist with is arms and pulled her up to her knees.

Jonah marveled at the firm perfection of her ass. He slid his dick along her slit to coat it in her juices and then rammed it home into her tight little ass in one quick motion. She jumped and gasped in surprise as his abdomen slapped her ass.

His erection was still rock-solid and her pain-filled little cries fueled the fires of his lust. He was relentless. Lena didn't know what to think. She was near tears, but also so turned on she was about to cum again. Submission had taken hold of her, and she both hated and loved what he was doing.

Jonah made one last thrust and she thought it would split her in two. She cringed at his growl of satisfaction. She thought he would cum soon, but she wasn't that lucky. The control she thought she'd have tonight had completely disappeared, and mild-mannered Jonah had become an animal.

Lena could tell he was nearly out of his mind with lust, and his need to cum had to be overpowering. He finally pulled his cock out of her ass and slammed it home into her pussy.

Lena was both relieved and shocked by Jonah's latest invasion, but her pussy had a mind of its own and gripped him tight. She needed release, so she rubbed at her clit with a shaking hand, adding this sensation to the rough fuck Jonah was delivering.

When her climax hit, wave after wave shook her body, and cries of satisfaction edged with pain escaped her lips. This was too much for Jonah, who fucked her even harder, driving the cum up from his balls so he could fill her to overflowing. When he finally came, they both collapsed onto the bed. The sexual tension they'd been fighting for months had been released.

Lena woke the next morning feeling better than she had in a long time. The stress she'd been living with for months was suddenly gone and she felt like a new woman. She stretched, yawned and reached over to caress Jonah to see if he wanted a repeat performance. Instead of touching his sexy body, her hand brushed a piece of paper.

Thinking he'd left a note about going to get breakfast or something, she smiled and started to read:

> *By the time you read this, my things will be out of your house and you won't have to worry about putting up with me for another minute.*
>
> *I don't like liars, but thanks for last night, it was a good ride.*
>
> *Jonah*

What the hell? She reread the note and still couldn't figure out what had happened. *Does he know? … How much does he know? Shit! I should have known better than to get my hopes up. I knew last night was too good to be true.*

Lena did the only thing she could at this point— she had a good cry. Once she was cried out, there was nothing left to do but move forward. *Get your ass out of bed, get yourself together and go have lunch with Sue. You have some damage control to do.*

Chapter 22

L ater that day, Lena heard her office door open and close but she didn't turn around. She knew it was Sue, because she'd gone to get some food for lunch so they could eat and gossip about their dates. Lena really didn't want to hear about Sue's date, but she also didn't want Sue to know what went on with Jonah. She was afraid of what it might mean for the Foundation's project with him.

When Sue still hadn't said anything after a few seconds, Lena knew something was off. It wasn't like Sue to stay silent for that long when there was juicy gossip to discuss. Lena turned around and froze. "What are *you* doing here? I thought you got what you wanted and you were gone for good."

"I changed my mind. I decided there were some things I needed to say to you."

"You called me a liar and pretty much treated me like a whore, so I really don't want to talk to you — ever," she said, barely concealing her rage and hurt.

"Well, *Sky*, you *are* a liar," he said, glaring.

Shit. He figured it out. I really didn't think it would make him this mad though, Lena thought as the fury radiated off him. "When did you figure it out?"

"My mother let it slip. Why didn't you tell me? Did you have some grand plan to hurt me or blackmail me or something?"

"No, Jonah. It was nothing like that."

"Then why?"

"I hadn't planned to tell you at all at first. I figured you didn't want anything to do with me in the past when I was Sky, but I needed you to work with me now as Lena. After working and living together, I realized that you were different than I'd imagined and I decided I wanted to tell you — I just didn't know how. I was afraid of how you'd react. Though I never imagined you'd react like *this*."

"Are you sure it wasn't that you were worried I wouldn't finish out your precious contract? It's hard for me to believe you since I told you about Sky and how I thought of her as my angel. Hell, I even called you my angel at the concert to try to give you an opening to come clean. You could have said something then, but you chose not to. I don't care what you say, I get the impression you were going to take that secret to your grave.

"I was in love with Sky. It damned near killed me when she just disappeared!" he yelled, raw emotion coloring his words.

"*You* were the one who disappeared! I called and wrote to you. I left voicemails until the number stopped working, but you never called or answered my letters. I even talked to your manager a couple of times, then her number stopped working too. You left me, so can you really blame me for not wanting to bring that all up again?"

"No. You're not going to make me the villain in this little story. This is all on you!"

"But that's what happened. We had that wonderful night together and then you disappeared. I got a couple of short notes from you that practically screamed I had become way too needy, then I never heard from you again."

"You're a liar. I wrote to you and you stopped writing to me. I don't like being played," he said as he turned to leave.

"Where are you going?"

"I'm going to talk to Nicole, my ex-manager, to see if your story matches hers. You'd better not be lying or your precious Foundation will suffer for it."

After Jonah left, all Lena could do was stare out the window. She didn't know whether to be sad or hopeful. *On one hand, JJ, my JJ, is gone and he's never coming back. The man who stalked out of my office is so far from being JJ that it's hard to believe they are the same person,* she thought. *I always secretly hoped there was a misunderstanding and JJ actually loved me. But, he's so different from the person I knew — so angry and paranoid.*

My sweet, thoughtful first love has turned into a bitter, angry and cynical man. I guess I never thought about what he went through after that wonderful night, because I couldn't believe that it meant anything to him. I mean, we had that night together and after that he just wasn't t he same. Then he disappeared.

He had all that money and all those people working for him, but he couldn't be bothered to be the one to track me down? Did it wound his giant celebrity ego to think that I was the one who walked away. Is that why he couldn't be bothered to find me?

Sue finally came back with two huge bags of food for lunch. "Sorry it took so long. That place was swamped, but I had my heart set on their pad Thai, so I stood in line like the patient woman I am not."

She proceeded to unpack the bags and completely cover Lena's desk in food cartons. "I wasn't sure what you'd like, so I got a bunch of stuff," she said as she grabbed her pad Thai and opened some chopsticks. "You okay? You look a little lost."

"It's nothing. I was just thinking. ... So, are you going to tell me about last night or am I going to have to pry it out of you?"

"I think I should make you suffer a little longer," Sue said as she stuffed her face. "I'm starving. Grab some food and give me a minute.

"Starving, huh? So, maybe there was a lot of physical exertion involved in your evening?"

"Shut up and eat," she said, smiling like the cat who devoured the handsome celebrity canary.

Sue was so happy about the date with Alex, so Lena didn't want to rain on her parade by telling her what went on with Jonah. She acted like everything was fine and told Sue that her date with Jonah was something she'd never forget. *That's true,* Lena thought, *but I'm sure she's thinking I mean something completely different from what really happened.*

Hell, I'm not sure what really happened. Did he believe me when I told him I tried to stay in touch? That lying, evil bitch Nicole! I can't believe I trusted her. She seemed like a responsible business woman who had Jonah's best interests at heart. I guess she wanted him all to herself. There's no point in dwelling on it now. The past is in the past. I can't do anything about it now. I just wish he would calm down enough to hear me out.

The rest of the day crawled by, and Lena was out the door at five on the dot. *If I have to spend one more second pretending everything is fine, I'm going to explode!* she thought as she hurried to her car.

All she could think about on the way home was a tub full of bubbles and a big glass of wine ... maybe the whole bottle. *I'll get a little tipsy and then I can sleep like the dead. That way, I won't have to think about anything.*

Chapter 23

When Lena walked into the house, she went straight to her bathroom and started filling the tub. She added lots of lavender-scented bubble bath to help her relax, then went to the kitchen to grab a chilled bottle of wine and a glass. She began undressing as she walked back to the bathroom, leaving her shoes, skirt and blouse on the floor as she went.

The bathroom was beginning to get a bit steamy, and the tub looked inviting, so she climbed right in and poured a big glass of wine, then set the bottle on the side of the tub. She had a feeling she was going to need the whole thing.

The water was hot and felt wonderful on her tight muscles. *Stress is really doing a number on me,* she thought as she shut off the tap and turned on the jets so she'd be completely boneless and relaxed by the time she got out. She grabbed a towel off the shelf by the tub, rolled it and put it behind her neck so she could lay back and close her eyes for a while.

She'd just started to drift off when a horrible racket nearly made her jump out of the tub. *What the hell is that?* she wondered, her little relaxation bubble completely ruined. The noise came again, accompanied by someone yelling. It sounded like someone was beating on the front door and screaming their heads off.

She reluctantly climbed out of the tub, dried off and put on a robe as she walked to the door. *I am in no mood for bullshit this evening. Hopefully they're at the wrong house.*

She looked through the peephole and was surprised to see Jonah standing there. "Open up, Lena. I know you're standing there looking at me."

"What do you want? You made yourself perfectly clear earlier. You don't need to insult me and tell me how evil I am. I heard you the first time and I know how you feel, so you can just go ahead and leave."

"Open the door, Lena. I need to talk to you."

"Well, I'm not in the mood to talk — especially to you. I can't take any more today, Jonah. Just go away." *Ugh, the nerve of this fucking man!*

"I'm not going to yell at you," he said in a softer tone. "Let me in. Please?"

"Why, so you can angry fuck me again to make me pay for my supposed transgressions? I don't think so. Goodbye."

"I was wrong to do that. I'm sorry."

"Yeah, apology not accepted," she said and slammed the door in his face.

"I spoke to Nicole today!" Jonah pleaded. "Please hear me out. I just want to explain."

Fuck! Why can I never just be done with this man? she thought as she flung the door open and glared at him. "Fine. Say what you need to say and leave."

"No, this isn't something I'm going to talk about while I stand on your front step," he said as he practically marched into the

133

living room and dropped down onto the couch. "Come in here and sit down, so I can talk to you."

She closed the door, trudged into the living room and stood there glaring at him.

"Go ahead and sit down. This is going to take a while."

"Fine," she said as she took a seat in a wing-backed chair that was as far away from Jonah's seat on the couch as she could get without going into another room.

"You could sit closer," he said with a small smile that quickly faded when she continued to glare at him, "but I guess where you are is okay too."

"Quit stalling, Jonah. You interrupted a relaxing bath and now I'm tense and stressed out again. Just say what you need to say."

"I came to say I'm sorry—"

"For what?"

"That I didn't believe you when you said you tried to stay in contact. I tracked down Nicole — she hasn't been my manager for a while now — and she told me what she did.

"She wanted you out of the picture, so she made sure I never got your messages or letters and she never sent the letters I wrote to you. A lot of things make sense to me now. For example, why I suddenly had to get a new phone and move into a fancier place, and why she started acting more like my secretary than my manager. All of that was so we couldn't contact each other. As I think about it now, I can see how she was manipulating me. I'm not sure why I didn't see what she was doing then.

"Part of it was that she had control over everything in my life, and I allowed that to happen. It was easier, so I just let her do it. Then, after you quit writing, I was miserable and heartbroken, so I just didn't really care about anything.

"As time went by, she convinced me we were meant for each other, and it seemed like the truth because she was so in tune with me. She knew everything about me and made sure I always had what I wanted, sometimes before I knew I wanted it.

"At first, I was flattered and I liked it, but eventually it became stifling. It was kind of like living with a detective because she was always watching me — always there, hovering and fussing. The more I tried to be independent, the closer she got. She was jealous, and it got to the point where I couldn't even speak to another female without her acting like a lunatic.

"When I got the balls to finally break it off, I had to file a restraining order to keep her away from me. She kept breaking into my place, leaving me gifts and notes. The final straw was when I got home one night and found her handcuffed to my bed. That was when I finally called the cops and filed charges.

"She ended up in behavioral health court after that stunt, and was sentenced to the maximum three years of program participation and treatment.

"I hadn't talked to her since then, until today. By the time we finished talking, she actually thanked me for filing charges. Can you believe that? She stole our happiness and she wanted to thank me for her punishment."

"Well, I'm glad you know the truth. Now, if you don't mind, I've had a long day and I'm tired."

"Wait, there's more I need to tell you."

"I really don't know if I can take anymore today, Jonah. Can't you save it for another time?"

"No. I need to tell you now, before things get more screwed up than they are."

"Okay, go head and get it off your chest."

"Even though I was heartbroken and thought you didn't want anything else to do with me back then, I still loved you. Then, I fell in love with you again, even though I didn't realize who you were. Even when I thought you were trying to trick me into working for your Foundation to help you expand your career, I couldn't help but love you. I've finally realized that I'm a lost cause — I'm going to love you no matter what. The big question on my mind is, do you love me the way I love you?"

Lena stared at him for a few seconds, trying to process what he'd just told her. *Am I dreaming?*

"Lena, don't keep me in suspense? Do you love me?"

"I never stopped. Even when I thought you just used me for sex and dumped me, I couldn't stop. I kept writing letters to you, even though I knew I'd never send them. Pretending to write to you was the only thing that got me through the dark times that followed.

"I even still loved you when I thought becoming Jonah Parker the celebrity had wiped away most of the sweet JJ I'd known. Initially, I didn't like present-day you, but I still loved you. I'm surprised you couldn't see it on my face every time I looked at you."

"I was blind and stupid. Can you forgive me?"

"I need some time to process this. My emotions are all over the place. I'll call you, maybe tomorrow, and we can talk, but right now I need space and time to think."

Lena showed Jonah the door. "I'm sorry, but it's just too much to deal with right now. I will call you … I just can't deal with anything else today," she said as she slowly closed the door.

Chapter 24

O h, my God. I regret making him leave already! Lena thought as she leaned against the closed door. Finally, she zombie-walked back toward the bathroom and her wine. *I want to believe his story, but can I trust that he's telling the truth or is this some game he's playing so he has another chance to get even with me? He was so angry before, now suddenly he's all apologies. I need to call Alex. He knows Jonah better than anyone, and I know he'll be straight with me.*

"Hey, Alex. Are you busy?"

"Lena, I was just thinking about calling you. I'm done for the day. How about I come over? We've got some stuff to talk about."

"You don't even know the half of it. I'll order us a pizza. See you in 20?"

"You got it."

Lena grabbed the wine and her glass and went to her bedroom to throw on some clothes. *Alex will know what I should do,* she thought with relief, as some of the tension left her shoulders.

Alex got there just as the pizza arrived, and paid for it before coming inside. "Hey, baby girl. You doing okay?"

"I'm better now, seeing you and that pizza," Lena said, chuckling as she took the box from him and headed to the kitchen.

"So, tell me all about your date with Sue," she said, unwilling to dive right into the Jonah issue.

"I don't know if I should, since you set me up."

"Don't be mad at me. I had good intentions. She's had a thing for you forever, and I thought you two would hit it off. Did you?"

"She's great. After I got over the shock of you ditching me, we had a pretty good time together. You did hurt my feelings, though. I really wanted to do something special with you. I thought that date would be my chance to prove that we needed to take things to the next level."

"Alex, and I love you — just not the way you want me to. I've never really loved anyone but Jonah. I think, deep down, you know that."

"Yeah, I guess I do, but I really wanted the chance to change your mind. Anyway, you meddling jerk, after I got over being pissed at you, Sue and I did have a good time together. What about you and Mr. Parker?"

"We had a nice evening … I thought maybe we were finally going to get a chance to be together again, but I was wrong. Shortly before the concert the other night, his mom told him who I really am. Apparently, he tried to give me an opportunity to come clean that night, and when I didn't he felt betrayed. I really thought his mom was going to give me more time to tell him myself, so I never suspected that he knew.

"So, held in his anger for days and by the night of the auction he was ready to explode. Believe me when I tell you, he was furious. What I thought was romantic, slightly rough lovemaking was really a revenge fuck on his part. He left me a note that thanked me for 'the ride." I found it on his pillow when I woke up the next morning."

"Wow. I don't know what to say. That doesn't sound like Jonah. He must've really been hurt."

"Him? Wait, are you taking his side in this? I wanted to talk to you because I thought you'd be on my side and make me feel better."

"You know I'm always on your side, but I also won't throw Jonah under the bus. I owe him my life."

"What? How do *you* owe him your life?"

"You don't know the whole story about my friendship with Jonah.

Chapter 25

"The me you know today isn't the person I've always been," Alex said. "I'm pretty content with myself and my life now, but it wasn't always that way. I'm the black sheep of my family — the one who didn't do what was expected of him. Instead of going into the family business, I became an entertainer. That was a pretty big slap in the face for my family."

"Your family's not in the mob, are they?"

"No, something much worse — they're all doctors. Don't laugh, doctors are way worse than the mafia, believe me."

"If you say so, but it doesn't sound that bad to me."

"Well, it was and still is — I've just learned to deal with it and separate myself from their disappointment. My family name is Maloney, you know like Maloney International Medical Group—"

"What? That's a multi-billion-dollar business. They're always in the news for doing something philanthropic or for inventing some new type of medical equipment."

"Yeah, that's them. You're looking at the former heir to the Maloney fortune. My childhood was miserable. It was dictated by my father's business schedule and doing all the things that made us look like the perfect family. We were about as far from perfect as you could get; no one was happy. But hey, we were rich, so I guess personal happiness didn't matter."

"What's this got to do with Jonah? His family isn't rich."

"I'm getting to that. You just need some background so you know where I'm coming from and why things went down like they did."

"Okay, I'll shut up and listen."

"Thanks. This isn't easy for me, I haven't really told anyone about any of this. ... I was in high school when I realized the only time I felt real joy was when I was performing. It didn't matter if I was making a joke at a party or giving an actual performance.

"I still felt that way when I was ready to graduate from college. As I said, I had money, so I hired a college pal to help me make a professional looking portfolio, then I told my parents I wanted to be an actor and I would not be following the family tradition of going on to medical school. Needless to say, that announcement *did not* go over well and they gave me an ultimatum — go to medical school or be disowned. So, I took the money I had in my personal account, bought a one-way ticket to LA and changed my name to Alexander Malone.

"The money I left home with was nothing like what I was used to, but I was determined to succeed. I found a seedy studio apartment and bought a beat-up Ford Fiesta so I'd be able to make it to auditions.

"I was pretty realistic for someone fresh out of school, and I knew I'd have to have a job to get me through until I got acting gigs. I still had my rich kid wardrobe, so I applied for a bar-tending job at the Ritz Carlton. I looked like I fit in, and I spoke their language, so they hired me on the spot. I was really lucky.

"I can't imagine you tending bar."

"Why not, it's kind of like performing. Plus, I got to meet all sorts of people with interesting stories, mannerisms and speech patterns, as well as people with important Hollywood connections. It was kind of like my own personal acting school and talent agent all in one.

"Anyway, the bar job was great because it left days open so I could go to every audition possible. I continued bar-tending for a couple of years without getting much in the way of parts, and even though I knew a lot of industry people I was beginning to think I'd made the wrong choice.

"It was depressing, so I started popping a couple of pills here and there to make myself feel a little better. Pretty bar patrons were always offering me that type of candy, so it was easy to just partake from time to time.

"More time went by, and I got a few acting jobs but nothing big, so my recreational use started to be an all the time thing. I was probably one step from becoming a full-blown addict when I met Jonah.

"He had a certain presence — strong enough that it made an impression through the drug haze in my brain. We talked quite a bit that night, and I realized he was a loner who was kind of lost, just like me. For some reason, I decided he should come with me for open mic night at one of my favorite spots. I was off on Thursdays, so we made plans to meet there.

"He'd told me he was a singer, so I figured he should get used to LA crowds by getting up there and singing during open mic night. So, when we got to the club, I made him add his name to the sign-up sheet for the night.

"He wasn't even nervous. He just got on stage, introduced himself to the band, said something to the guitar player and the next thing I knew Jonah had the guy's guitar. When he started to play, no one really paid much attention, but then he started singing and that changed immediately. By the time he finished the song, the crowd was yelling for more. He just smiled and said he didn't want to take more time than he was due, put down the mic and left the stage.

"Most performers have to be dragged off the stage, and he willingly gave the mic to the next performer. It was such a non-LA thing to do that it made me respect him more and gave me a glimpse into the type of person he was. You don't meet many like him in LA.

"He got off the stage and started to look around for me, so I stood and motioned him over. He smiled and nodded, then started making his way to my table. Before he got halfway across the room, I watched a guy stop him and talk to him for a minute. Then he handed Jonah his card, and I knew I had just seen someone get their big break. It was right out of a movie script.

"I mean, can you believe that our trip to that club on that night coincided with Andrew Bennett, one of the biggest music producers out there, being in the audience? Jonah Parker is one of the luckiest people I've ever met!"

"This is a great story and all, but I already knew this — all but your part in it. You know about my obsession with the man. This is doing nothing to make me think I can trust him. It's pretty much making me think he's Teflon and nothing bad sticks to him for long."

"I'm not done. Just listen and learn."

"Fine."

"The next six months were what every budding musician dreams of. Jonah signed a big record deal, and his whirl-wind rise to celebrity status began. He started releasing singles online, and his PR people quickly worked that into a million-plus followers. After that, he started getting radio play, and then came the TV interviews and eventually his first album. I know you know all of this, but I was there with him, every step of the way.

"He was getting everything I'd ever hoped for, and he basically didn't have to work for it. This just made my depression worse and my self-esteem was at an all-time low. I did a pretty good job of hiding it though, being an actor and all.

"That all came to an end when I OD'd. If Jonah hadn't been worried and come to check on me, I'd be dead. He got me to the ER and then stayed with me until I came around."

"My God, Alex, why didn't you ever tell me this?"

"I was ashamed and I really didn't want you to think less of me. Jonah is the only one who knew about this, until now.

"I came clean with Jonah. I told him how depressed I was and how sick it made me that I was jealous of his success. And do you know what he said?"

"No, what?"

"He apologized to me because he didn't see what was happening sooner and help me before it got so bad. How crazy is that? I'd just told him what a horrible person I was, and he apologized for being busy with his life and not noticing what was going on with *me*. That kind of behavior was completely foreign to me. No one in my family, with all of their doctor egos, would have ever said something like that and meant it like he did.

"What's even more incredible is he thought, and still thinks, that I'm the reason for his success — just because I invited him to that club and made him get up on stage. He's probably the least self-centered person I've ever met.

"He told me he was going to pay for me to go to the best rehab in LA, and then when I got out I was to move into his new mansion with him. He said I could live there as long as I wanted. Hell, he even paid off the lease on my crummy apartment.

"When I got out of rehab, he was true to his word and had one whole wing of his house made up for me. What's even more unbelievable was he was looking for work for me. He was a total celebrity and he was job-hunting for me — a nobody. Hell, he even found me a high-powered agent.

"Eventually I got my first major TV gig. It came with a two-year contract and a nice yearly salary. I wouldn't be rich, but I wouldn't have to live at Jonah's anymore either. That was the first step to my own celebrity status, and it was all because of Jonah Parker and how much he cared about our friendship.

"During the time I lived with him, I got to know the Jonah no one in the public ever gets to see. I found out he wasn't a completely happy person either. In his unguarded moments, I could see the sadness lurking just below the surface. I asked him about it more than once, but he wasn't ready to talk about it.

"Now that I know more of the story, I suspect that sadness was related to t the way you disappeared from his life and some leftover guilt about his relationship with his parents. I think he's always loved you, and he never really got over losing you. You know he's only been with one person since then, and that didn't last very long."

"His ex-manager, Nicole?"

"Yeah, she had it bad for him and did everything she could to be exactly what he wanted. The problem was, he'd already had the one he wanted and anyone else was just second best."

"If that's true, then we've both wasted so much time. So many lies and secrets, mostly on my part. Do you really think we can get past all of that and have something real?"

"Well, baby girl, I think that's totally up to you."

145

Chapter 26

After Alex left, Lena decided she was going to take a chance and try to find the happiness she'd always hoped for. *I just hope he's willing to give it a try too,* she thought as she called him.

"Ms. President, it's late. Have you found some portion of our contract I haven't fulfilled? I can't imagine you'd be calling for any other reason."

"No, I've called to apologize. Do you still want to talk? I hope so, because there are some things I need to explain."

"Why the sudden turn around?"

"Well, a very wise man told me I was stupid not to trust you because you're the most trustworthy person he knows."

"Oh, really? And you believe him?"

"I do. He's my best friend. I believe he's your best friend too."

"Ah, so Alex has been whispering in your ear. You realize he's in love with you, right? Maybe you should take what he says with a grain of salt."

"No, he told me the truth. He's a loyal friend to you, and I think he's got a better idea of what's going on than we do. He knows I love him, but I made it clear to him that it can never be in the romantic way he wants."

"And why is that?"

"Because I love you. I've always loved you, pretty much from the moment I heard you singing at the hospital. Since that time, you've never been far from my mind — even when I was mad and hurt and thought you'd dumped me."

"If that's true, then why didn't you tell me who you were? You had lots of opportunities."

"It took me a long time to come to terms with you ditching me after we slept together. It nearly destroyed me. Between that and all of the terrible things going on in my life at that time, I have some deep emotional scars and a lot of trust issues."

"How could you think I'd just dump you after we'd been writing to each other all that time, and sharing all our hopes and dreams? Did you really think I was that kind of person?"

"Well, you were rich and famous and had women throwing themselves at you all the time. Why would I think I could compete with that? I was a nobody and you were a star. I figured you got what you wanted from me and ignoring me was a convenient way for you to get me out of your life. I mean, I was hardly the type of person a megastar should have a romantic interest in.

"Plus, I tried to stay in tough. I wrote and called and even tried to track you down. I knew you knew right where I was but you never tried to contact me. What was I supposed to think?"

"I did try to contact you, but the woman who answered your phone said you didn't want to talk to me, and the letters I sent to you were never answered. It seemed pretty clear to me that you wanted nothing to do with me."

"I never got any letters from you, and Selena confiscated my phone. … I can't *believe* she didn't tell me you called. She knew

147

how miserable I was. That's probably why she didn't tell me — she's always enjoyed my misery.

"Oh, my God, Jonah. I can't believe those two awful women are the reason we've both been through all this torment.

"Would you like to read some of the letters I wrote to you?"

"How can I do that?"

"Well, some of the ones I mailed came back with address unknown stamped on them. Also, I was in the habit of using you as my sounding board, so I just kept pretending to write to you, sort of like a journal, because it helped me work thorough everything that was going on in my life. Doing that was the only thing that kept me sane for a long time. You can come over and read a few of them if you want. After that, maybe we can talk?"

"Yeah, I think I'd like that. I'll see you in a bit."

Jonah sat on the bed looking at the letters Lena had picked out for him. She wanted him so see she wasn't lying about writing them, but didn't want him to read them all. She just couldn't deal with that right now, because it might ruin everything.

Instead of reading them to himself, Jonah started reading out loud:

"Dear JJ... Wow, I haven't heard that name in years. You were the only one who got to call me that. It was kind of my secret identity that only you knew about.

He went back to reading the letter, "Hey Superstar, I can't tell you how happy I am to know that your career is going so well. I've given up being mad at you for leaving me and moving on. I need you too much to give you up completely, so I'm going to keep writing to you. I hope you don't mind.

"My life sucks. I hate living with Selena, but it won't be for much longer. I'm moving out soon and heading to college. I can't wait to be away from here. I can't get away from Mommy Dearest Selena and her drugs and revolving door of men fast enough. She isn't thrilled about me being in her life again, either. She thought she'd ditched me for good when Gram took me off her hands, but now she's stuck with me again because Gram died. Plus, she's mad because she didn't get the inheritance she was expecting.

"I just keep a low profile around her, like Gram told me to do. If Selena ever figures out that Gram tricked her and left her money to me, I'll be in a world of hurt. I can't thank Gram enough for making sure I can get away from Selena and go to college without having to worry about how to pay for it. She's still protecting me from the grave. I just don't know how such an extraordinary woman could give life to a woman like Selena.

"Thanks for listening. I always feel better after I've written to you. Hope your new album hits number one! Ever Yours, Sky.

"God, Lena, I'm so sorry you had to go through that by yourself. I'm so pissed at Nicole right now—"

"Look, it's in the past and there's nothing we can do about it. Let's just move forward and find something good together. That's the best way to get back at her."

"You're right, but that doesn't make me any less pissed," he said, turning to the next letter.

"Dear JJ—"

"You really don't have to read them all, especially not out loud. I know what they say."

"I want to be able to comment about what I'm reading, and I like reading them aloud," he said, then continued.

"Well, I've finally gotten away from Selena. I doubt I'll ever see her again. I can't really say I'm sad about that. But I am sad that I'm pretty much alone in the world now.

149

"I've got a tiny apartment a few blocks from campus, and my classes start today. Things aren't going to be easy, but I'm looking forward to learning everything I can.

"Apparently, I'm more nervous about this whole move and starting classes than I thought I'd be. I've lost my appetite and this morning I barfed before I headed off to my first class. I guess it's normal to be this nervous, but I hope I get used to it soon. I hate throwing up.

"I've been reading the tabloids and see that everything is going well for you. You're really living your dreams. I'm so happy for you. I'll write more later. Ever Yours, Sky.

"Were you really that nervous about classes?"

"Yeah, I hate to fail and there was every chance that I might. No one in my family had ever gone to college before."

"Well, you certainly got over the insecurity, since you graduated top of your class and became the successful Ms. President sitting in front of me today."

"I did get it figured out."

"Wow, this one's a short one," he said as he came to the next letter.

"Dear JJ, I talked to your manager, Nicole, today. She promised me she'd get a message to you. I really need to talk to you. It's important. I don't know what I'm going to do and I really need you right now. I hope I hear from you soon.

"I'm getting pissed again," he said as he turned to the next to last letter in the stack. "This one's short too.

"Dear JJ, I didn't hear from you, so I talked to Nicole again today. She wouldn't give me your cell number, but she gave me your address. I'm going to write you another letter right now and drop it at the post office. I hope I hear from you soon.

"She either intercepted it when it came to the house or she gave you the wrong address. I never got this letter, you have to believe me. "

"Again, it's water under the bridge, so let's just forget about it. Please?"

"I don't know that I can do that. Let's see what this final letter says.

"Dear JJ, I sent the letter, but I still didn't hear from you. I'm pretty sure it got to you because that one wasn't returned. I guess you don't really care what I do, so I'm going to do what I feel is best.

"I've got some soul-searching to do, so I probably won't write for a while. Ever Yours, Sky.

"Wow, I can tell you were getting a little angry with me as time went on. I'm so sorry things happened this way. You have to know that I would have been there for you, no matter why you needed me, if I'd known about it. So, what was it you wanted to tell me?"

Come on, Lena, now's your chance to tell him and get all the secrets out in the open.

"Lena, what was going on then? You sounded a little desperate."

"Look, it doesn't matter. There's nothing you could do now, so let's just drop it. Okay?"

"For now, but eventually you need to tell me."

"We'll see. I just don't want the ghosts of the past to ruin what we might have in the future."

"You mean you're willing to consider a future…with me?"

"Of course, I am. You're the only one I've ever really loved. I just never thought it would be possible."

"What about your former boyfriend? What was his name?"

"I thought I cared about Ash, but now that I look back at our relationship I think he was just a convenient way for me to forget about you. I needed someone in my life — I didn't want to be alone anymore — and he happened to be there. I stayed with him way longer than I should have ... but that's in the past too."

"Well, how about we start building a future, together?"

"I'd like that, but I'd also like to take it slow. You know I have trust issues, and I think it would be better if we made a fresh start and got to know each other without the past influencing us. We could pretend we just met."

"I can work with that. ... Ms. Walker, would you like to go on a date with me? Maybe tomorrow evening? We could have dinner."

"Why, Mr. Parker, I think that sounds lovely."

Chapter 27

Three months later

"I've got a surprise for you," Jonah said as Lena joined him for lunch at their favorite restaurant.

"I'm not a big fan of surprises."

"Oh, I think you'll like this one."

"Well, don't keep me in suspense. You know I don't like to wait either."

"Oh, believe me, I know," Jonah said, chuckling. "I'm moving to Atlanta! I bought a house almost two months ago, and the renovations were finished a few days ago. That's where I went when I left your house."

"*What?* That's great. How did you find a place so fast?"

"Our friend Alex hooked me up with his Realtor and she found the perfect place right away."

"When can I see it?"

"We can drop by after lunch if you want."

"Of course, I want to. I can't wait to see it. What about your place in LA?"

"There's nothing and no one holding me there. I've already put it on the market. It's a nice place, so it should sell pretty fast."

"This is a big change for you. Are you sure you want to move so far away from all the movers and shakers?"

"I've done a lot of thinking since *someone* made me come here, and I realized I want to be closer to the people I love. That includes you. So, yes, I'm sure."

"Really?"

"I know you worry about losing people when you love them, and because of that you're afraid to allow yourself to fully love people. I'm asking you to take that chance with me."

"Jonah, you know I love you, but I *am* afraid you'll hurt me … or leave me again. I haven't really had anyone in my life I can depend on to be there for me, other than Gram and Alex. Trusting doesn't come easy for me."

"You have more than just them. Once upon a time, you had me too. Let me be that again, angel, and I promise, no matter what, I'll never leave you for any reason."

Lena was so shocked that she just sat there, saying nothing.

"You know what? Fine, go be with Alex. Apparently, he's the only man on the planet worthy of your trust," Jonah said, misinterpreting her silence.

"It's not like that, you idiot. I love Alex because he's my best friend. He's been there for me every time I've needed him. I wouldn't be the person I am now without his influence in my life.

"I know how he feels about me, but I've already told you, I don't feel that way about him. He's not happy about how I feel, but he understands and loves me enough to want to be a part of my life, even if it means only being friends. Besides, I have a feeling he will be pretty occupied with a certain lady in the very near future."

"So, does this mean you think you can trust me enough to let your guard down and be with me fully?"

"I'm willing to try."

"I'm so glad to hear that, because I have a question for you. I was going to wait, but it feels like right now is the perfect time to ask."

Jonah got up from the table, pulled a ring box from is jacket pocket and got down on one knee. He opened the box with a flourish, and asked, "Helena Sky Walker, will you do me the honor of becoming my wife?"

His question was met by stunned silence.

"Lena? Oh, my God, why are you crying?"

"Because I'm so happy," she sobbed. "I feel like I'm dreaming. If I am, I never want to wake up!"

"No, you're not dreaming, and you haven't answered my question."

"Yes! Of course, my answer is *yes!*"

Jonah put the two-karat yellow diamond ring on her finger, stood up and kissed her. "You've made me a very happy man."

"Shit! I can't stop crying," Lena said, dabbing at her eyes. "I'm happy too. Do you think we can get out of here before I make more of a scene?" she asked as the other patrons near them started clapping and congratulating them.

"Sure. Let's go tour my new house. We can see if it meets with the future Mrs. Parker's approval."

Chapter 28

The doorbell rang early the next morning as Lena was rushing around trying to get ready for work. She'd spent the night with Jonah at his new house, and had rushed home to shower and change. She looked out the window and saw a car she didn't recognize. When she got to the door, she peered through the peephole and hesitated. *What the hell is* she *doing here?*

"I know you see me. I'd really like to talk to you, if you don't mind," Jonah's mother said from the other side of the door.

I wonder if she's going to try to talk me out of marrying Jonah. Might as well find out if this is going to be a battle. "Good morning, Mrs. Parker," she said as she swung the door open wide. "Won't you come in?"

She came in and just stood there, not saying a word. "May I get you some coffee?" Lena asked, trying to fill the awkward silence. "I was just about to have some."

"Yes, that would be great," she said, following Lena into the kitchen, and taking a seat.

"I've always wanted to thank you, you know."

"For what?"

"For being you and for being there when Jonah needed you most. If you hadn't come along when you did, I don't think he would be here with us today."

"Really?"

"Yes. I believe what happened that day at the hospital was God's will. People are placed in our lives for a reason, and you were there to ensure Jonah stayed in this world. You can't tell me you don't believe in fate. Especially when you've been brought back together in such an extraordinary way.

"I'm sorry I let your secret slip, but I'm glad I did. I'm not sure you would've ever got up the nerve to tell him yourself. ... I wish you had reached out to us when you couldn't get in contact with Jonah. We could have saved you both so much hurt and suffering."

"I had really low self-esteem at that point in my life, and I convinced myself that he wanted nothing to do with me. I just couldn't take the chance that you would feel the same way."

"Well, you know different now. Right?"

"Yes, I think I finally do. Did you know he asked me to marry him yesterday?"

"Yesterday? He told me he was planning some fancy candlelight dinner. Guess he couldn't wait. That really doesn't surprise me."

"His proposal was a complete shock, and I can still hardly believe it."

"Oh, believe it, sweetie. He loves you. He's been happier these last few months than I've seen him in a very long time. I think you're going to be a wonderful daughter-in-law. We can't wait until you're a part of our family."

"Thank you. I'd love that more than anything. I haven't had a family since I lost Gram."

***

Chapter 29

Jonah's mother left after their short conversation, and Lena went to work, feeling better about things. She'd gone straight to Sue's office and shared her good news, and showing off her beautiful engagement ring.

The hours flew by, and just as she was finishing up for the day, Sue popped into her office and asked, "You ready to dish, now? I've waited all day to get all the details about how that gorgeous ring ended up on your finger."

"I'll tell you everything, if you finally give me *all* of the details of your night with Alex. He won't tell me anything juicy because he says he doesn't kiss and tell."

"Deal. Let's get out of here and go someplace where we can get food and booze."

"Let's go to that little pub down the street. We can ask for a table in the back so we can talk."

"Okay, food and booze are ordered, now tell me about you and Alex."

"Well, he was a little peeved about your bait and switch. I think he felt rejected and more than a little embarrassed."

"I know. I got that much out of him. I apologized and explained why I did it. He's okay with it, I think, even though what I did was pretty selfish. In reality, he's probably still a little pissed at me, but he'll get over it thanks to you."

"Well, I'm pretty sure it's going to take him some time to get over his crush on you."

"I know, and every time he brings it up I tell him that I love him like a brother. I can't help the way I feel, but I realize he can't either. I just don't want to lose him. His friendship is really important to me."

"I know, and he knows that too. He's just hurt. It probably wouldn't be such a bad thing if he found someone who loves him back..."

"And you think that someone is you?"

"Yeah, I do. We had a wonderful night and I think there's a real connection there. If he can just get you out of his system, there just might be some room for me."

"Well then, you need to be persistent and shove thoughts of me right out of his head!"

"Trust me, I'm working on it!"

***

Lena's phone rang as she got home from the pub. "Jonah! I'm just walking through my door. Want to come over?"

"Sure, babe. How was girl's night?"

"It was great. Sue's hatched a plan to make Alex notice her in a romantic way. I hope he's smart enough to recognize what a great woman she is."

"I don't know, sometimes Alex has a hard time getting out of his own way. You and I may have to give him a shove to help Sue out."

"Yeah, you may be right about that. He's still kinda mad at me, so maybe I can fix that and talk Sue up at the same time."

"Sounds like you have your battle plan all put together."

"So, do you want to come over tonight? It's lonely here all by myself."

"I would love to, but I'm actually headed to the airport. The Realtor called this afternoon and told me there's a buyer who wants the LA house and he wants to get the deal done as quickly as possible. I thought about asking you to come with me, but I know how you are about missing work."

"It seems like you know me too well already. I definitely couldn't take time off right now. I hate it that you're going to be gone though. This whole engagement thing feels like a dream, and I need you here in person to make it feel real."

"I'll be back in a few days, and then you won't be able to get rid of me."

"I can't wait. Will you call me when you land, and then keep me updated on how things go tomorrow?"

"Try and stop me. You'll probably be telling me to quit bothering you because I won't be able to leave you alone."

"I wouldn't have it any other way."

"I love you, future Mrs. Parker. It seems like I've been waiting my whole life to have you by my side."

"I love you too, Jonah. Have a safe flight and call me when you land — no matter what time it is. I won't be able to sleep until I know you're safe."

"I'll talk to you soon, love."

Chapter 30

L ena woke up the next morning and ran for the bathroom to be sick. *Ugh! That greasy pub food definitely did a number on my stomach,* she thought as she washed out her mouth and looked into the bathroom mirror. *Oh, God, I look like shit. Maybe it wasn't the food and I'm sick instead? I don't have time for this. I've got too much work to do.*

She showered and put on some makeup. *Better,* she thought as she looked at her reflection in the mirror and applied some lipstick. *At least I don't feel like puking again, but I feel like I could sleep for a week. I am not good when I don't get a full eight hours.*

The work day flew by and Lena managed to get a lot done, even though she still felt a little drained. She'd stayed busy, so she hadn't missed Jonah too much. *That's probably because he called five times and sent about 10 texts,* she thought and smiled. *It's so nice to have someone including me in their life like that.*

Sue came bursting through her door, interrupting her pleasant thoughts. "Since Jonah's MIA, what the hell are we doing tonight? I could definitely eat."

"As long as it's not that pub again, I'm game. I had a bad reaction to that food."

"I'm feeling barbecue. What about you?"

"Sounds good, and I know just the spot. You'll love it, trust me."

Thirty minutes later, they arrived at a hole in the wall restaurant. The place looked a little iffy, but Lena knew they served the best barbecue in the area. *"I'm starving,"* Lena thought as she looked over the menu.

"Sheesh, where are you going to put all that?" Sue asked, after the server left with their orders.

"I skipped lunch because I was still a little nauseous, and now I feel like I could eat a horse!"

"This I have to see. You usually eat like a bird."

"Whatever, I'm going to pig-out. Spill, I know you've got juicy news. It's written all over your face."

"Alex called me last night," she said then squealed like a little girl.

"What did he say?"

"He asked me if I'd like to go on a real date instead of a date he'd planned for someone else."

"I'm assuming from the un-Sue-like squeal you said yes?"

"Of course, I said yes. I'm *not* crazy."

"Well, I expect a full report from you. I need to make sure my two best friends are doing things right."

"You'll get every sexy detail, I promise. I plan to show Mr. Malone just how much I like him."

"That sounds interesting. I can't wait to hear all about it."

"Your turn, girl."

"My turn for what?"

"You're practically glowing today. What's up?"

"I'm just so happy. Jonah called and texted me all day today, keeping me up to date with how his day was going. It's such a nice feeling, having someone care about me enough to do that."

"Oh, my God. It's so romantic and sappy. I have to admit, I'm jealous. You've got it all — career, a celebrity best friend and a handsome, famous fiancé. It's a little rough being in your shadow. You're a tough act to follow, considering the man I want has placed you on such a high pedestal."

"What are you talking about? You're gorgeous, successful and you've got a date with one of the most handsome celebrity men on the planet. You aren't in anybody's shadow."

"Yeah, I guess you're right about that. But can I still be jealous that you get to plan a wedding?"

"A wedding? Ugh! I don't even want to think about that."

"What? Why not?"

"I don't have any family to invite, and my only two friends will be part of the wedding party. You will be my maid of honor, right?"

"Are you kidding? Of course I will!"

"I'm so glad. It wouldn't be the same without you. As far as a big wedding goes, I don't think that's in the cards. Jonah has his parents and maybe a few extended family members, but he doesn't really have anyone he actually cares about, other than Alex, to invite either. So, there's no reason to plan some big, flashy wedding if we have to invite a bunch of show biz people we don't care about. I was thinking something small, maybe at my house in the rose garden, so it will feel like Gram is a part of the ceremony. That was always her favorite place."

"That sounds nice, actually. But, you still need a dress, and I'll need something pretty too. We should hit the boutiques."

"I was hoping maybe I could wear one of your originals. Everything you make is so beautiful."

"You'd really want me to make your wedding dress?"

"You're an amazing designer. Why wouldn't I want to wear an original Sue creation?"

"Wow. I'd better get busy then. I'm going to make you the best wedding dress ever."

"Nothing too fancy. I'd rather have something classic and simple."

"I've already got the perfect design in mind. Let's head to my place, after I watch you eat ten tons of food, so I can get some measurements."

"Sounds like a plan."

Lena's cellphone rang just as she coming home from Sue's house. "Hello?" she answered, without checking the caller ID.

"Hello yourself."

"Jonah! How's the real estate deal going?"

"It's done and I'm on my way to your place. I just left the airport."

"How'd you get here so fast?"

"A friend was coming to Atlanta and offered me a ride in his jet."

"Must be nice to have friends like that!"

"Oh, it is, baby."

"Very funny. Have you eaten or do I need to try to throw something together for you?"

"I had something on the plane — that flight was first class all the way."

"That's actually kind of good, since I'm not sure I've got any actual food here. You might have been stuck with a peanut butter sandwich."

"I'm not above a good PB&J once in a while."

"Good to know. How far away are you?"

"I should be at your door in twenty."

"Great. I'll see you then."

True to his word, Jonah rang the doorbell 20 minutes later, and Lena got up and eagerly went to let him in. When she opened the door, she smiled at Jonah and then crumpled to the ground.

"Lena? Lena, come on. Wake up, baby," Jonah said as he knelt, cradling her head.

"What happened?"

"You opened the door and fainted. I didn't realize the sight of me was so shocking," he said, chuckling while looking worried.

"I just felt a little lightheaded, and next thing I knew I was on the floor and you were telling me to wake up."

"Has this happened before? Were you feeling sick earlier or anything?"

"I had a stomach bug yesterday, but I felt great today. I must've got up too fast and got lightheaded."

"Well, I think you need to see a doctor. Let's go to the ER and get you checked out."

"No, I'm fine. I don't want to spend the night sitting around the ER waiting for someone to tell me what I know — I'm fine."

"Well, I guess I can't force you to go, but will you please make a doctor's appointment tomorrow and get yourself checked out? This isn't normal and I'm worried about you."

"I promise, even though it's a waste of time."

"Humor me, soon-to-be Mrs. Parker. I don't want anything to happen to you."

"Fine, fine, you win. Now, help me up off the floor and tell me how the sale went."

Chapter 31

"Remember to make that appointment," Jonah said the following morning as he was leaving.

"What appointment?"

"The one you promised you'd make with your doctor. You're not getting out of that. You need to make sure you're okay."

"Fine, but I probably won't be able to get in for at least a week. You know how doctor's schedules are."

"I don't care. Just make an appointment, and then go to it."

"Okay, Mr. Bossypants. Just because I'm wearing this beautiful ring doesn't mean you get to tell me what to do."

"Ha! Like anyone could ever boss you around if you didn't want them to."

"Yeah, you're right about that."

"Hey, want to have a lunch date today? We could go to that place on Piedmont that has the lobster fried rice you like."

"That sounds great."

"I'll see you at noon. ... Make that call!"

I'm way too busy to fit in a doctor's visit. It'll be a waste of time I don't have, Lena thought as she went to shower and get ready for work. Halfway to the bathroom, a wave of nausea hit and had her running to make it to the toilet in time. *Okay, doctor's appointment it is.*

Once she felt better, Lena looked up her doctor's contact info and called. "Hi, this is Lena Walker. I'd like to make an appointment, please."

"Hi, Ms. Walker. You're in luck. We just had a cancellation. If you can make it in at ten this morning, we can fit you in today."

"That's great. I'll see you then."

I hate doctor's offices and exams and everything else involved. I hope it's just some virus so I can get back to work in time to meet Jonah. These paper gowns are ridiculous, Lena though as she waited for the doctor to return with the results. *Wonder if I can just get dressed while I'm waiting...*

There was a knock at the door, and the doctor breezed back in, interrupting Lena's rambling thoughts. "Ms. Walker, I think we've figured out what the issue is."

"That's great. Do I have a virus or some kind of stomach flu?"

"No, I'm afraid it's simpler than that. You're pregnant."

"What? I can't be. I've got an IUD. It's impossible."

"Well, the impossible has happened. There's no mistaking the results. We'll need to remove that IUD, too."

"Are you sure?"

"I'm sure. How about we do an ultrasound so you can see for yourself?"

"Okay ... yeah. Let's see."

"Go ahead and lie back on the table. We'll just do a quick ultrasound. That should show us what we want to see," the doctor said as he applied the gel to the vaginal wand.

"Looks like this is a healthy pregnancy. No complications from the IUD," he said, viewing the monitor. "The baby is just fine. See, that tiny blip on the screen right there? That's your baby."

"Oh, my God. I'm pregnant."

"Do you have a primary obstetrician?"

"No. I wasn't supposed to get pregnant. How did this happen?"

"Well, you're in the one percent of women who get pregnant despite using an IUD. You might say you were destined to be pregnant, if you believe in that sort of thing."

"Destiny or maybe someone up there figured out I was about to get everything I've ever wanted and decided to throw a wrench in the works."

"I'm sure once the shock wears off you'll be able to think about this more clearly. But for now, we need to go ahead and remove the IUD."

"Do whatever you need to do, doctor."

"Let me go get things ready. You can just lie there. We can perform the procedure right here."

"All done, Ms. Walker. Everything went well with the removal and I don't foresee any complications from the IUD. I'm going to go ahead and give you a prescription for prenatal vitamins that you should get filled today. I would recommend you find an OB/GYN as soon as possible."

"Okay, doctor."

"Are you sure you're going to be okay to get yourself home? You seem a little out of it. Do you need to call someone?"

"I'll be fine, thank you."

Chapter 32

L ena made it into her office without having to speak to anyone. She closed the door and slumped against it. *God, why now? Couldn't you let me have just a little time to enjoy the happiness before you threw me a curve ball? Shit, every time I have sex with Jonah Parker I get pregnant — two times, two babies. Shit!*

A knock pulled her from her thoughts and she opened her office door to find Jonah standing there. "Wow, is it lunchtime already?"

"Yes, it's actually almost one o'clock. You okay? You look a little off."

"Um, yeah, I'm fine. Let me grab my purse and we can head to the restaurant."

"You sure you're okay," Jonah asked as he hurried to follow Lena as she made a mad dash out the door. "When is your doctor's appointment?"

"I went this morning. They had a cancellation and I got right in."

"Great. What did you find out?"

"Can we wait to talk about that until we get to the restaurant? I need food immediately."

"Um sure, I can wait. We'll order, and then we can talk about what the doctor told you. Apparently, you weren't okay, like you thought."

"Okay. I can't wait any longer," Jonah said after the waiter walked away to place their orders.

"I'm basically fine."

"But…"

"But, I'm also pregnant."

"Pregnant?"

"Yes, around three months. I know exactly when it happened, and so do you."

"Pregnant?"

"You're going to have to say more than that, or I'm going to start crying. I didn't do this on purpose. I had an IUD; this was *not* supposed to happen."

"But somehow it did?"

"Yeah, apparently about one percent of women who use IUDs end up getting pregnant. Lucky me."

"You're going to have a baby … *my* baby?"

"Yes. It's your baby. I haven't been with anyone else since I left Ash. It couldn't be anyone's but yours."

"Wow … a baby … guess it's a lucky thing I asked you to marry me. Right?"

"You don't think I did this to trap you, do you? Having a baby right now is *not* something I wanted, though I had hoped for that somewhere down the road."

"No, of course I don't think that. I guess I'm just in shock. This was the last thing I expected you to tell me today."

"It was the last thing I expected too, believe me."

"I guess this means we should speed up our wedding plans. It would be nice to be married before he or she gets here. Not to mention we don't want the tabloids to tell the world about our baby news before we tie the knot — it might damage my wholesome reputation," Jonah joked.

"Oh. ... I hadn't even thought about that. I'm not used to worrying about reporters caring about what goes on in my personal life. Guess I'm going to have to get used to that along with everything else that's about to change."

"That *is* one of the pitfalls of being famous — nothing is private anymore."

"Well, let's keep our wedding as private as possible then. I was just telling Sue I think a small ceremony at my house would be really nice. We can invite only the people who are important to us and not do anything too fancy."

"You mean you don't want one of those 'celebrity-style' mega weddings that are so popular with the in-crowd right now?"

"That's actually the last thing I want. We've been through so much, and it's all been traumatic and stressful for both of us. Our wedding should be something we can both enjoy, not some circus for the general public's entertainment."

"I'm so happy to hear this. I was really dreading dealing with a big, flashy wedding," Jonah said with a relieved smile. "Guess all we need to do now is decide on a date."

"I would say the sooner the better. Don't you think? The longer we wait, the more likely it is someone from the press will figure out our secret. The only thing is, I've asked Sue to make my wedding dress. I'd really like to wait until she can get that done. Her designs are amazing."

"Why don't you let her know our plans and what we're up against and see if she can work faster? In the meantime, I'll find out about the wedding license, get someone to officiate and see about hiring a caterer. You think Alex would be my best man, even though he's been in love with my bride-to-be for years?"

"If Sue's plan works, I don't think you'll have to worry about him pining over me anymore. So, I think he'll be happy to be your best man."

"Sue's plan sounds interesting and maybe a little dangerous for Alex," Jonah said, chuckling.

"So, you're really okay with everything?"

"Of course, I am. I love you, and now that the shock has worn off a little, I'm excited about welcoming a new Parker to the world in a few months."

***

Chapter 33

"Wow, you're eating standing up? Couldn't wait to dig in until you sat down at the table, huh?" Jonah asked as he came up behind Lena and wrapped his arms around her, caressing her flat belly.

"This little human can eat! I woke up this morning and the only thing I could think about was pancakes with a ton of syrup."

"Don't worry, I'll make sure you get as many pancakes and anything else as you want, little one."

I feel like I've stepped into someone else's life. This has been my dream since before I got his first letter in the mail, Lena thought. *I can't believe I'm here with this man and freaking pregnant with his baby. Again! God sometimes has a really twisted sense of humor when it comes to what He has in mind for me.*

"So, I'm off to set things in motion for the wedding," Jonah said. "I want you to take it easy. No more fainting! I don't want anything to happen to my future wife or that little person baking in there," he said, caressing her stomach fondly.

"I'll be fine. I'm going to stop by the pharmacy and pick up the prenatal vitamins the doctor prescribed, and then I'm going to the office."

"You need to minimize stress, young lady. Have you told Sue you're pregnant?"

"No. I didn't want to tell anyone before I told you."

"That was nice of you. You need to tell her now so she can help you with work when you need it."

"Listen to you, trying to boss me around again. I hope you realize that marrying me does not mean you get to tell me what to do.. There will be no bossing me around unless I get to boss you too," Lena said, laughing as she turned around to face him.

I've never been as happy as I am at this moment, she thought as she looked up into Jonah's eyes, and then kissed him like her life depended on it. Jonah didn't hesitate to kiss back, but he let Lena take the lead. The kiss deepened, and Jonah cupped Lena's ass with both hands, pulling her closer. *It's like we can't be close enough,* Lena thought with wonder.

Jonah moved the plate of pancakes over and lifted Lena onto the counter. He nudged her knees and moved to stand between them, while his hands roamed, leaving a burning trail everywhere he touched her.

Just as things were about to get interesting, Sue's ringtone blasted from Lena's phone.

"Ignore it," Jonah said gruffly.

"I can't. She's either calling about your final concert for the Foundation or about my wedding dress. Either way, I need to answer it or she'll just keep calling until I do."

"Fine. Tell her she has terrible timing! I'm going to go take a cold shower and then get out of here," he said, dropping a quick kiss on her lips and walking stiffly away.

"Sue," Lena groaned when she answered the call, "you don't know what you just interrupted."

"Hmm, were you having morning sexy time with that handsome financé of yours?"

"I was trying to, but *someone* called and interrupted us."

"Sorry, but you don't have time for that right now. I was up all night working on the toile for your dress."

"What the hell is a toile?"

"The linen version of the dress that I'll use as the pattern for the real one once we get it the way you want it."

"Oh. I didn't know you did that."

"Do you think I just wave my magic wand and a finished dress appears? That's not how it works. Anyway, I was up all night and I've got it done. I need you to come over and try it on so I can get the fit right and make sure you like what I came up with."

"Are you taking the day off today?" Lena asked, surprised.

"I think we both should. Today should be all about your wedding."

"I think you're more excited about this than me, if that's possible. But, when my boss says to take the day off, I'm certainly not going to say no."

"Good. Now, how quick can you get over here? I can't wait to see this on you."

"I need to shower and get dressed, and then I'll be on my way."

Sue opened the front door before Lena even got out of her car, motioning for her to hurry up.

"You really are excited for me to try it on, aren't you?" Lena asked, smiling at her friend as she walked inside.

"Yes! This is the prettiest thing I've ever designed and I can't wait to see what it looks like on you."

"Well, I won't make you wait any longer. Where is this master-piece so I can model it for you before you give yourself a stroke?"

"Follow me. I'll help you with it. This version is pretty flimsy, but it will tell me what I need to know so I can make the perfect dress."

"How long do you think it will take before you have the real dress finished?"

"I don't know. Why?"

"Well, Jonah and I decided we want to have a really small wedding and we want to have it as soon as possible."

"Really? Any special reason why?"

"Well, yes, that's the other thing I wanted to tell you. I went to the doctor yesterday, and—"

"You're not dying, are you? Oh, my God, you've got some incurable disease—"

"No! It's nothing like that. It's life-changing, but I'm not dying … I'm pregnant."

"*What?*"

"Yeah, apparently one night with Mr. Jonah Parker is all it takes to defeat nearly infallible birth control."

"Wow. Does Jonah know?"

"Of course, he knows. That's part of the reason we want to have the wedding so quickly. He wants us to be married *before* the baby is born. It's kinda sweet that he cares so much."

"Never thought I'd see that."

"What?"

"Lena Walker being all sappy about love. It's kind of weird."

"Very funny. Now, help me put this thing on so you can get to sewing, woman."

177

After a bit of a struggle, the dress was on and Lena was shocked by how beautiful it was — even in its plain muslin form. "You've outdone yourself, Sue. This is amazing."

"Thanks. I think so too. It's kind of surprising, because this is probably the fastest I've ever come up with a design — I didn't even really have to think about it much — I just started cutting pieces and it went together without a hitch."

"I don't want to seem like I'm rushing you, but realistically how long do you think it will take to make the dress?"

"I would say probably two weeks, if I take some vacation time and work on it exclusively. I really want to use this antique lace I've had forever to add some detail to the dress. That will add some extra time to apply, but I think it will be worth it."

"I can't ask you to take vacation time to make my dress. Surely we can keep this a secret for longer than two weeks so you have more time to get it done without burning your vacation days."

"I wouldn't count on this staying secret, especially if anyone spots that rock on your finger and sees the two of you together. It wouldn't take a genius to figure things out. I don't mind doing this for you. If it makes you feel better, this can be my wedding gift to you."

"Oh, Sue, you're the best friend ever! How can I ever thank you enough for doing this for me?"

"You can say you're okay with me wearing one of my existing dresses as my bridesmaid's dress. That way I won't have to make something new for myself."

"Well, that's a not a problem. You can wear whatever you want, as long as you're standing up there beside me."

"It's settled then, you can tell Jonah he's only got three weeks left as a free man."

"I thought you said two weeks."

"Let's build in an extra week. That way, we have a little time to deal with any emergencies that might come up."

"I'll tell him as soon as we're done here. Now, I've got one last thing to tell you, and I hope you're okay with it. ... Alex is going to be Jonah's best man."

"Oh, girl, that's not a problem at all. That's actually perfect. You know I've been working on seducing that man. This will give me another opportunity to get back in his pants. He won't be able to resist me in the dress I'm planning to wear."

"You're a diabolical and evil mastermind," Lena said, laughing. "He doesn't stand a chance. It shouldn't be long before I'm standing next to you when you're wearing your wedding dress!"

"That's the plan, my friend, that's the plan," Sue said, wearing a huge grin.

***

Chapter 34

Lena was feeling the pressure of pulling off a wedding in just three weeks. Time had flown by in a whirlwind of planning, choosing a menu for the reception, and making personal invitations to those invited to the wedding, since all of the guests had to be sworn to secrecy.

"What do we have left to do before the big day? We've only got a few days left, you know," Lena asked at breakfast.

"I still need to get the wedding license. I think I should do that today, just in case there's some red tape we have to clear up or something. I'd hate to have a piece of paper stop us from getting married."

"Great. I've got one last fitting with Sue and my dress should be done. I can't believe how quickly she got it put together. Have you rented a tux?"

"I don't need to rent one. I own a really nice one, and Alex said he'll go with me this afternoon to pick up the Merlot colored cummerbunds Sue told us to order. Apparently, that's an 'in' color and will coordinate with her dress and your bouquet."

"Yeah, she can be a bit bossy when it comes to that stuff. I didn't really get to choose the color of my bouquet — she told me what needed to be in it to work with our dresses."

"Well, I guess it's good you didn't have to agonize over what to choose with her being the style dictator," Jonah said, and chuckled. "I don't really care about the clothes or the colors, as long as I get to put that ring on your finger and make it official."

"You know, I feel exactly the same way. Are you sure Alex is okay with being your best man?" Lena asked for the hundredth time. "He really hasn't talked to me since you asked him. I've been giving him his space, but it's making me crazy. I don't want to lose him as a friend."

"I think he's doing just fine. He's been taking dinner to Sue every evening while she's sewing your dress, and I think she's worked her magic on him. He's quit acting like a whipped puppy about losing you to me and he seems to be pretty happy. I don't know what Sue's doing, but she needs to keep doing it."

"That's great to hear! I want them both to be happy, and I know Sue honestly cares about *him*, not his money or fame."

"Maybe you need to reach out to him. He might feel awkward about calling you."

"I think you're right. I'll call him later and thank him for helping you get things ready and keeping Sue fed while she sews."

Later that morning, Lena was at Sue's again, trying on her dress. "Lena, I think we're almost done," Sue said happily. She'd been fussing over the final details of the wedding dress since Lena put it on.

"It looks amazing. You are *so* talented!"

"Thanks, it is pretty darned gorgeous, even if I do say so myself. I should have all the last little details finished in the next day or so, and you already have the shoes … so, I think you're ready in the dress department. Have you made an appointment at the salon?"

"Yes, and I made one for you too, and the stylist and makeup people will be here at 9 a.m. sharp the morning of the wedding."

"In that case, let's get you out of this dress, then I'll get my phone and see if my favorite spa has an opening. We both need a spa day!"

Chapter 35

L ena woke up the following morning, and the first thing she saw when she opened her eyes was Jonah. He was still asleep, and he looked so peaceful. *Damn, that man manages to look good even when he's sleeping.* She tried to slide out of bed without disturbing him, but the minute she put her foot on the floor, his eyes popped open. "Where are you going, gorgeous?"

"I was trying not to wake you."

"How are you feeling this morning?"

"I feel wonderful. That spa day was worth every penny. I'm buffed and polished everywhere."

"That's good, because at this point there's no way you're getting out of marrying me," he said with a big grin. "Sorry I had to interrupt things to drag you over to the courthouse yesterday. I had no idea you had to be there with me before they'd give us a marriage license."

"It was no big deal. Sue had so many things scheduled for me, it was nice to take a little break. A girl can only stand so much pampering at one time."

"Really?"

"No, but I didn't want you to feel bad."

"How about I make you and our baby some breakfast to make up for it?"

"That actually sounds good this morning. This is the second day in a row that hasn't started with me immediately barfing my guts up. I have my fingers crossed that I'm done with the morning sickness stage."

"Glad to hear that," he said with a chuckle. Why don't you shower and get dressed while I play chef?"

"I'll see you in a bit."

A little while later, Lena came into the kitchen to find a frowning Jonah. "What's wrong?"

"I just got off the phone with my publicist. The tabloids know we're getting married."

"*What? ...* How?"

"I had no idea the local paper checks for new marriage licenses and publishes them weekly. Apparently, someone at the paper is tipping the tabloids off about anything involving me, and they jumped right on the story. I'm sorry. The paparazzi will probably be driving you nuts as soon as they figure out who you are."

"Oh well, the wedding is in a few days and they don't know a thing about that. As long as we can keep them away from our day, it will be fine. I knew I would have to get used to the media circus because you're so well-known, I just hadn't planned on that happening until after we tied the knot."

"Maybe you can stick close to home until after the wedding? I don't think there's any way they know about your house or that I stay here pretty much all the time. You'll probably be safe from them for a while if you stay here."

"I guess it's a good thing all of the planning and running around is done."

"You sure you still want to marry me? You're probably in for a lot of hate mail from my female fans."

"I think I can deal with that, but they need to realize there's only so much of you I'm willing to share with them. They get the rock star, but I get the rest."

"You certainly do."

***

Chapter 36

The day of the wedding dawned bright and clear. The caterers arrived at 9 a.m. and started setting up, and Sue was right behind them with the dresses. As soon as she walked in and spotted Jonah, she started pushing him out the door. "You can't be here, mister. You can't see Lena in her dress until she's walking down the aisle."

"What? Nobody told me that. Where am I supposed to go?"

"Go to my house. Alex is already there, and you two can help each other get dressed. Just be sure to call and warn us before you leave to come back here so we can make sure you don't see your bride."

"Fine. I can't believe you're throwing me out of here on my wedding day."

"Get over it. You'll be back soon enough. Now scoot. I've got a lot of work to do," Sue said before hurrying off to Lena's bedroom with the dresses draped over her arm. She laid the dresses out on the bed and went looking for her best friend. "Lena, where are you?"

"Sue, is that you already? I'm in the bathroom brushing my teeth. Give me a minute."

"Well, hurry up. We've got a lot to do and not much time to get it done. The hair and makeup people will be here any minute."

"Wow, you're bossy when you're stressed. I think you're more nervous about this wedding than I am."

"I just want everything to go right for you two. It's taken a long time for you guys to get here."

"It will be fine, so stop worrying and just enjoy. Besides, I'm not the only one getting her way today," Lena said, winking at her best friend.

The doorbell rang, interrupting their banter. "They're here!" Sue shouted. "I'll let them in while you decide where they need to set up shop."

What seemed like an eternity later, the women both had hair and makeup done to perfection. "Come on, I want you to put on your dress so I can be sure I don't need to make any last-minute alterations," Sue said, bubbling over with excitement.

"Okay, but you're going to have to help me so I don't ruin anything."

"Lena, you look beautiful," Sue said with tears in her eyes once the dress was on. "You're the prettiest bride I've ever seen, and I'm not just saying that because you're wearing my creation. You're stunning, but you look a little pale."

"Yeah, I'm nervous all the sudden. We've been so busy getting everything in place so we could make this happen that I didn't really have time to think about anything. It just all kind of hit me, and it's a little overwhelming."

"You'll be fine. Once you see Jonah standing up there with the minister, it will all be worth it and you won't be nervous anymore."

"I hope you're right. I'd hate to throw up at my own wedding."

"Well, that would certainly make this ceremony memorable."

"I don't think I want that kind of memory."

"You'll be fine. Come on, we need to get in place. The music is about to start. It's almost show time. Let me grab my phone and I'll check to see how the guys are doing."

"Sure. I'm going to check mine to see if I have any messages and then I'm turning it off."

Hmm, that voicemail is from an unknown number. That's weird. It's probably a telemarketer, but I'd better listen to it just in case:

> *Well, ain't you something gettin' engaged to that celebrity boy? I couldn't believe it when I saw your face on the TV. You didn't even tell your own momma. Just like you didn't tell me you were back livin' in my house. I did some checkin' and I never could find a way to get it away from you. I can't believe that old cow left it to you instead of me. It should be mine!*

> *I'm gonna bet ya haven't told your new man about your little secret, you know the one that came along about 15 years ago. You didn't think I knew about that, did ya? I'm not stupid. I knew you was pregnant when ya moved out.*

> *I bet it's worth a pretty penny to you to keep that quiet. Your new man probably thinks you're all high society and shit. He probably wouldn't want to marry ya if he found out you're a slut with a 15-year-old kid out there somewhere.*

> *So, here's what you're gonna do. You're gonna give me back my house and you're gonna pay me*

*$10,000 a month for the rest of your life. You'll have
plenty of money once you marry that rich celebrity,
so you won't miss what you're payin' me.*

*If I don't hear from you in three days, I'm gonna
find that man of yours and tell him all about you.*

I knew all of this happiness was too good to be true, Lena
thought, panicking. *I should have known something would come
along and ruin it for me — I just never imagined it would be
Selena. What am I going to do? I'm so close to my happily ever
after. I'm marrying Jonah today, no matter what. I going to have
the one thing I've wanted more than anything, even if it only lasts
for three days.*

The walk down the aisle was surreal. *All I can think about is
that damn voicemail. Why couldn't she just leave me alone? I can't
believe Selena is trying to blackmail me. ... Stop it! Lena, now is
not the time to be thinking about this. You're getting married to the
love of your life.*

Lena snapped out of her depressing thoughts as she looked
at Jonah standing there waiting for her with her two best friends
on either side of him. *He looks so handsome!*

"Jonah and Lena have asked you here today to witness their
union," the minister said, once Lena came to stand next to Jonah.
"The couple has written their own vows, so we'll start with Jonah."

Lena handed her bouquet to Sue and turned to face Jonah. He
took her hands and said, "Lena Walker, love of my life, the day I
met you, my life changed forever. I've never known a woman like
you. I look at you and I know that I am truly blessed, and that
God really does have a plan. From this day forward, I vow to be
your best friend, your protector, and your partner in everything

you do. We were destined to be together. I love everything about you and that love is forever. Today, you're making me the happiest man alive. I love you, angel," he finished and slid the wedding band onto her finger.

"Jonah Parker," Lena began, "I look into your eyes, and see JJ, the boy I fell in love with all those years ago. I've dreamed of this moment for a very long time, and now that it's finally here I'm happier than I've ever been in my life. You are my joy, my love, and from this day forward, I vow to be your partner in every way. Second chances don't come around every day, but somehow we've managed to get ours. I vow to cherish you and live every day of the life we share to the fullest. You are the love of my life," she concluded as she slid the ring onto his finger. Once it was there, a feeling of peace came over her.

"By the powers vested in me by the state of Georgia," the minister said, "I now pronounce you husband and wife. You may kiss your bride."

As they kissed, Lena thought, *I wish this moment could last forever.* Smiling from ear to ear, the couple turned to face their guests and got a round of applause.

"We did it, Mrs. Parker," Jonah said as they walked back down the aisle together. "There's no getting rid of me now. I'm here for the long haul."

"I hope you know what you're getting into, Mr. Parker, because I have a feeling life with me is going to be a bumpy ride."

"What's that supposed to mean?"

"Oh, nothing. I'm so happy I'm talking nonsense. Let's go get some food. This baby of yours is letting me know that I skipped breakfast."

"Your wish is my command, oh wife of mine."

Chapter 37

"You make a beautiful bride," Alex said as he came to stand next to Lena. "I'd always kind of hoped you'd be mine, but I realize now that it was never meant to be."

"I'm sorry I couldn't be what you wanted, Alex. You know I love you and you're one of the most important people in my life. I don't know what I'd do without you."

"I know. I'm wonderful," he said, and chuckled. "Just not as wonderful as Jonah Parker."

"Don't be a jerk, it's my wedding day."

"Oh, I'm not. I'm just being truthful."

"Alex, you are extremely wonderful, but I was in love with Jonah before I even met you. I think maybe you thought you loved me because I cared about the real you instead of the celebrity. I know that's a rare thing in your profession. I'm just sorry I didn't make it clear to you sooner. I was selfish and I'm sorry."

"I accept your apology, and I think maybe you're right. I was lonely and you 'got me' in a way no one else had, until now. I think I've found someone who really is the one for me. She flusters me and challenges me, plus she looks at me like I make her world go around."

"Oh, Alex! It's Sue, isn't it? I hope it's Sue. She's crazy about you."

"Of course, it's Sue. Who else would it be? We spent a lot of time together working on your wedding stuff, and now I find myself thinking about her any time she's not around. I think maybe I might be ready to take it to the next level with her and make our relationship something more than casual."

"Well, it's about time. The poor woman has been throwing herself at you from day one," Lena said, and chuckled. "I'm so happy for you!"

"Enough about me and Sue. We're here to celebrate your new life with Jonah."

"Speaking of that, I need to talk to you about something that's threatening my new life before it even gets a chance to begin. I'm going to need your help because I think you're the only one who will understand and not judge me."

"You know I'm always there for you, but this sounds kind of ominous."

"It is, unfortunately."

"Can it wait until tomorrow?"

"Definitely. Today is for celebrating!"

***

Chapter 38

"Good morning, Mrs. Parker."

"Good morning, husband of mine. Wow, that is both weird and wonderful to say."

"What would you like to do on the first day of our married life?"

"I think I'd like to stay right here where I don't have to share you with anyone."

"That sounds like a plan, but I think we'll eventually have to venture out into the world."

"I know, and I do actually have to talk to Alex about a time-sensitive project he's doing for me. I just don't want the world to intrude on our time together."

"That can be arranged. I can probably even manage a breakfast cooked by a sexy personal chef."

"Would he be shirtless and possibly look just like my husband?"

"That would be him."

"Could he possibly use an audience while he's cooking? I'd hate to miss all that sexiness in action."

Laughing, Jonah got out of bed and threw on some joggers and a tee shirt.

Lena took a long moment to admire his muscular back and tight little butt. "Hmmm, that view is making me hungry, but not necessarily for food."

"Mrs. Parker, you need to feed our baby before we resume any strenuous activities."

"Fine, but after we eat, I'm in charge."

"Yes, ma'am."

They headed to the kitchen, and while Jonah got busy cooking breakfast, Lena grabbed her phone so she could text Alex. Before she could get that done though, she noticed another voicemail from the unknown number and clicked to listen to it: *"Tick-tock, little missy. You've only got two days left before I tell."*

"Lena, are you okay? You look really pale all the sudden."

"Yeah, I'm fine. I think you were right. I need to eat something. I guess the chef had better hurry up before I pass out from hunger or something."

"Very funny. I'm almost done. Just waiting for the toast to pop."

"I think I'll survive. While I'm waiting, I'm going to text Alex."

"Fine, but that's all the work I want you doing today. We're on our honeymoon."

"Okay, *dear,*" Lena said, forcing a laugh as she texted madly:

> *Alex, I need your help. Can you set up an appointment for me with Aaron Banks, he's the attorney who handled Gram's will? He's in Atlanta. Jonah doesn't want me "working" today, so I can't do it. I only have 2 days to get things set and avoid that*

*threat I told you about. I know you're going to tell
me to talk to the cops when you know all the details,
but if this information gets out, it could ruin more
than just my life. It's worth it to me to keep it quiet.
I'll tell you everything later.*

"Here you go, my darling wife. Breakfast is served."

"Thank you, my amazing husband. It looks wonderful."

"So," Jonah began as he came back to the breakfast bar with his own plate, "what do you think about going somewhere on a honeymoon?"

"It sounds wonderful, but I don't think it's practical. We both have obligations. I wouldn't feel right just dumping things on Sue, and there are things you're scheduled to do that only you can do."

"I know, but I want some time alone with my new wife."

"That's sweet, but I don't think we should go away right now."

"Okay, if that's what you want. Just know that if you change your mind, we can be out of here and I won't look back."

"Well, maybe if you let me do some work today and tomorrow, I can get things squared away enough that I could manage to get away for a few days without feeling too guilty."

"Fine. I should've known I couldn't keep you away from work without a fight. You have two days, Mrs. Parker, then after that I'm whisking you away and we're going to enjoy a proper honeymoon before the world finds out we're married and comes knocking on our door."

Chapter 39

"Well, I guess if you're going to work today, I might as well get something done too. I'm going to make sure my schedule is clear for the rest of the month so we really can run away together."

"I'll work on doing that too. I'll talk to Sue. She'll probably be okay with it, as long as you're still willing to do that last concert for the Foundation."

"Even now, you're wrangling things from me for your job? You're incorrigible, Mrs. Parker."

"I know, but it's for a good cause. Plus, there's the added benefit of getting to see you perform. I never get tired of that."

"Flattery will get you everywhere. Of course, I'll be finishing out my contract with the Foundation. I mean, I could hardly disappoint its president, now could I?"

"No, you certainly couldn't," Lena said, smiling. "Let's get to it so we can meet back here and have a quiet evening together."

"You want to stay here or go to the new house? All of the furniture has been delivered and everything is move-in ready."

"If you don't mind, I'd like to stay here a few more days. It makes me feel closer to Gram, and being here with you is sort of like introducing the two of you. I know it sounds weird, but it makes me feel good."

"I'm all about making you feel good, Mrs. Parker. I'll meet you back here between five and six."

"Come over here and give your wife a kiss. That will have to hold me until I see you this evening."

"Happy to oblige, Mrs. Parker."

As soon as Jonah was out the door, Lena was on the phone to Alex. "Hey, it's me. I got Jonah to agree to let me deal with work for the next two days, so if you haven't had a chance to call Banks yet, I can do it."

"Already done. I called his office right after I got your text. It wasn't open yet, but I left a voicemail and got a call back at eight on the dot. I take it Jonah is out of the house?"

"Yeah, why?"

"I'm coming over and you're going to tell me everything. No more vague explanations. If you want my help, I need to know what's going on."

"Alex, I don't want anyone to know all the sordid details."

"Too bad. If you don't tell me, I'm not going to help you."

Lena sighed deeply, and said, "Fine, I'll tell you everything, but you have to swear you won't tell a soul."

"We'll see."

"No, you have to swear."

"Fine, but all bets are off if I think you're in any kind of danger."

"Get over here and I'll tell you everything."

"Were you already on your way over here when we talked? You got here in record time," Lena asked Alex when she answered his knock on her door.

"I may have broken some laws getting over here," Alex said, as they walked toward the kitchen.

"Have a seat, speed demon. I've got a lot to tell you and you'll need to be sitting down to hear it."

"Well, that sounds bad."

"Yeah, well. Here goes. The first part isn't too shocking, because you know a little bit about it. My mother is a narcissist and an addict. She never wanted anything to do with me, so Gram took me in when I was really young and she raised me. I hardly saw my mother, Selena, until after Gram died. I had to live with her in this house until I was 18. Selena never cared about me in any way, and she resented being forced to live with me. "

"I'm sorry. That must've been rough for you. Every kid needs a caring parent."

"Oh, I had that, it just wasn't my mother. Hell, I can't even stand to call her that. I've called her Selena since I was five or six years old."

"I assume this is going somewhere?"

"Yes, you needed to know the background before I told you the rest. The thing is, before I moved out to head to college, I was pregnant. I thought I'd hidden it from her, but she noticed."

"What difference does it make that she knew you were pregnant?"

"You don't know all the sordid details yet. Let me get it all out without interruptions or I might not be able to finish telling you."

"Okay. I'll keep quiet."

"I wasn't quite 18, I was pregnant and I was terrified. There was no way I was going to tell Selena — she's not the type of person I could confide in. So, I just acted like everything was normal and went off to school as planned.

"All this time, I thought I managed to fool her, but she knew I was pregnant and didn't mention it or offer to help me or anything. She wouldn't have benefited from helping me, so she just let me go off on my own."

"What a horrible mother... Sorry, I'll shut up."

"Yes, she *is* a horrible mother. Wait until you find out just how horrible she can be. Anyway, I loved the baby from the moment I got over the shock of finding out I was pregnant, and there was no way I wasn't having her.

"I did my homework and got Gram's lawyer, the one I told you to contact, to help me set up a private adoption. I wanted my baby to have a good life, something I wasn't sure I could provide being an 18-year-old single mother. It was an open adoption and the parents plan to tell her she's adopted at some point and let her decide if she wants to get to know me.

"I've kept tabs on her over the years and she's doing well. She's smart and athletic and beautiful. They did a wonderful job of raising her and I'm proud of her.

"This isn't about me being ashamed of *her*, it's about me being terrified that Jonah won't want anything to do with me once he finds out. Or worse, he'll want to do something that will cause problems for our daughter. We agreed there'd be no more secrets between us when we got married, but I just couldn't tell him this."

"I don't understand why you don't want to tell him."

"You promised you wouldn't judge."

"I won't judge, but you found out he didn't know. He didn't get your letters and it was all a big misunderstanding. Don't you think you should tell him now?"

"I'm being selfish. I finally have him in my life and he loves me. I just can't destroy that. I've wanted it for so long..."

"But he has a daughter he doesn't know about."

"*I know!* Don't you think I know that? Now Selena is blackmailing me. She doesn't know Jonah's the father, but she knows I haven't told him I have a daughter. She's going to spring it on him if I don't give her Gram's house and pay her $10,000 a month for the rest of my life."

"That's extortion! You can't let her do that to you."

"I have to if I want to keep my secret. I've been married for less than 24 hours. I'd like to have a tiny slice of happiness before Selena destroys it."

"You know, the longer you keep quiet the more hurt and upset Jonah's going to be. Right?"

"Alex, I'm terrified he won't want anything to do with me when he finds out. That's why I'm going to cooperate with Selena's demands, at least for a little while."

"So, why are we going to see your lawyer?"

"Because, I want to be sure someone official knows what's going on. That way, I can drop the hammer on Selena when the time is right. I'm not going to let her get away with it, I just want to do things on my schedule."

"Okay, but you need to tell Jonah. He has a right to know."

"I know that. Just let me be selfish and enjoy being married for just a little while before I ruin it. *Please?*"

"Fine. The appointment with your lawyer is in an hour. We'd better get on the road."

"Seriously? You could have said something sooner. Traffic is going to be terrible."

"You told me to shut up and let you talk. So, I obeyed," he said, laughing. "I wouldn't dare disobey a direct order from you."

"Mr. Banks, thank you for seeing me on such short notice," Lena said as she and Alex came into Mr. Banks' office.

"You know I'll always make time for you, Lena. Your grandmother was one of my favorite people. What can I do for you today?"

"First, I want to be sure that what I say here is bound by attorney-client privilege. You can't tell anyone what I say today, including the cops. Right?"

"That's correct. Have you committed a crime, Lena?"

"No. I'm being blackmailed."

"That's serious. Why don't you want to go to the police?"

"I don't want anyone to know what she's holding over my head."

"You know the blackmailer?"

"Yes. It's Selena, my mother."

"Your mother is blackmailing you?"

"Yes. I'm sure you have a pretty clear picture of the type of person she is, since you worked for Gram all those years. Selena's only out for herself. She thinks I'll be willing to pay for her silence about my secret for the rest of my life. I want her to think that I'm going to go along with it, and that's where you come in."

"What exactly do you want me to do?"

"I want you to help me build a case against her, so that when I choose to reveal the secret she's blackmailing me about I can bring in the law and press charges."

"I see. You realize she could get up to 10 years in jail for this, don't you?"

"Truthfully, I don't really care. She was never a mother to me and she obviously has no maternal instincts whatsoever or she wouldn't be blackmailing me."

"True, true. So, what were her demands exactly?"

"The deed to the house Gram left me and ten grand each month. She just found out I'm back living in Gram's house and she's still furious that Gram left it to me instead of her. Is there a way we can make it seem like I've transferred the deed to her without actually doing it? I think if I can convince her that I'm going to do that, she'll back off for a little while."

"I can draw up some paperwork and she'll have to sign it. You can tell her she has to come here to do that in front of me before the transfer can move forward. We'll have to have a witness to the signature and someone to notarize it. Those people will also be the witnesses who can tell the police exactly what they saw."

"That's good! The papers won't be official until you file them, will they?"

"No. You'd both have to sign and then I'd have to file the paperwork, which takes about 30 days —"

"You won't actually file anything though. Right?"

"That's correct. We can tell her things won't be official until the county accepts the filing and she can't take possession of the house for a 30 days. That will give you time to let the police in on what she's doing."

"Okay. One problem down and one to go. She's asking for $10,000 a month until the end of time. I can cash in my 401(k) and get that amount, but I don't know how quickly I can make that happen. Do you think I could get the bank to give me a secured loan for that amount by the end of business tomorrow?"

"Wait," Alex interrupted. "You don't need to do that. I'll loan you the money."

"No, Alex. You might not get it back. If I give it to her to keep her quiet for a while, I'm sure she'll spend it on drugs and booze and it will be gone. I can't let you do that."

"You can, and you will. I have plenty of money and I want to use it to help you."

"Lena," Mr. Banks said, interrupting the argument, "I can call the president at Citizens Trust, he's an old friend. I'm sure he can fast-track a secured personal loan for you today."

"That would be great. Thank you."

"I would suggest you use a cashier's check for the transaction. That way, there will be a record of what you've paid her."

"She may not like that."

"Just tell her it's as good as cash and she can redeem it at any bank for a small fee. Tell her it's the only way you could get that much money together on such short notice. Also, banks have to report withdrawals of $10,000 cash and you didn't think she'd want that."

"Oh, that's good. I'm so glad we came to talk to you, Mr. Banks. I'm feeling much better about how this is going to work out."

"I'll make the call to the bank, but Lena I still have to try to convince you to go to the police," Mr. Banks said. "It's never a good idea to cooperate with blackmailers."

"That's what I told her," Alex chimed in.

"I'm fully aware, gentlemen, but I'm going to do things my way. I'm not going to let this woman completely ruin my life — I'm going to bring her down. I just need to do it on my schedule."

"Well, since we can't change your mind, Ms. Walker, I'll see you on Friday at ten to sign the transfer papers. You should come about fifteen minutes early so we can be sure we have everything in place before your mother arrives."

Chapter 40

"*Your time's almost up, Missy,*" Selena said in a snotty voice when Lena answered her cell. "*Bring the first payment and the deed to my house to Big Daddy's at four tomorrow.*"

"I'm aware of the deadline, Selena. I'm getting the money from the bank in the morning, but the deed is a different matter. I saw Gram's lawyer today and he said we have to sign some paperwork in front of him and a witness, and then he'll have to file with the county and wait 30 days before the house can be legally transferred to you. I made an appointment with him for Friday morning to get that started."

"Figures you'd bring that shyster Banks inta this," Selena practically snarled.

"I didn't really have a choice. You didn't give me enough time to do anything else. This was the quickest way I could find to get it accomplished. Will it really hurt you to wait thirty days to have things done legally so that there won't be any question of ownership down the road?"

"I guess not, but you better not be tryin' anythin' underhanded."

"I leave all the underhanded stuff to you. This is all upfront and legal. He said he'd draw up the paperwork, then you sign, I sign and the witness signs. A notary will be there to stamp it and make everything legal. You wait 30 days for the county and that's all there is to it."

"Fine. You'd better be there with my money tomorrow right at four."

"I'll be there."

Oooh, that witch is a piece of work. If I wasn't so worried that Jonah will leave me when he finds out the truth, I'd be enjoying the fact that I'm tricking her.

The next morning Lena went to the bank and signed all the paperwork to get a $10,000 personal loan. "Thank you for getting this done so quickly, Mr. Prendergast," Lena said as she shook the bank president's hand. "I really appreciate that you personally handled it too."

"Not a problem, Ms. Walker. Aaron Banks is an old golfing buddy. I was happy to help out one of his clients. You just let me know if you need anything else."

"Thank you. Can I ask you a question? Will there be a record of who cashes this check?"

"Yes, it will come back to the bank once it's cashed and the endorser's signature will be on the back. You can even ask for a copy if you want it for your records."

"That's perfect. Thank you again for all your help.

One more trap laid for Selena, Lena thought as she left the bank. *I'm sure the cops will appreciate her signature on the back of that check. It's almost as good as putting "payment for blackmail" on the memo line!*

Next, Lena went to the sheriff's office. She had written down the dates and times for the texts and voicemails Selena had sent to her, and added the receipt for the $10,000 cashier's check to the list.

When she got there, a polite officer talked to her and explained what could happen. "Ma'am, this is actually a case of attempted extortion at the moment, not really blackmail under Georgia law."

"Okay. So, how do I keep it 'attempted' and not let her actually accomplish it?"

"Well, if you can get her to admit what she's trying to do and a law enforcement official is there to witness it, we can charge her, but I'm sure she'll try to fight it because no transaction will actually occur."

"What if a transaction happens, but it's not the one she thinks it is? Will that count as her completing the crime?"

"Yes, but you'll need to be careful and you'll need officers there to make sure you're safe, especially if you think this person might become violent."

"I've been working with my attorney, Aaron Banks, to try to keep her from getting what she wants. He's the one who told me to involve law enforcement. Do you think you coordinate something with him and arrange a setup so that you can catch her red-handed?"

"Mr. Banks has a good reputation around here, so I'm sure we can work with him to help resolve this problem for you."

"Excellent, just let me know what I need to do and I'll do it right away. I'm tired of this woman trying to ruin my life."

With the report filed and the specifics given to the police, all that was left to do now was wait until Thursday, when Selena would take the first step in sealing her fate.

Chapter 41

L ena walked into Big Daddy's Soul Food at exactly four. The aroma of well-prepared food greeted her, but anxiety was churning her stomach too much to allow her to enjoy it. She looked around the restaurant, spotted Selena sitting at a far table and walked directly up to her.

"Well, glad to see you can tell time. Where's my money?"

"Here," Lena said, thrusting the cashier's check at her.

"This ain't cash. I told you to bring cash!"

"Shh! You want someone to hear?" Lena asked as she sat down across from Selena. "You didn't give me enough time to get cash, so you got a cashier's check."

"What do ya mean? Just go in the bank and take out the cash. Don't take no time to do that."

"When it's $10,000 it does. The bank has rules about that and they keep a record of a withdrawal that big. I didn't think you'd want that, so I got a cashier's check. The bank teller said it's just as good as cash. Take it to any bank and they'll cash it for you."

"Fine, this time. You'll have a whole month to get it next time, so that had better be cash or I'm goin' straight to your man and tellin' him everythin.'"

"Whatever, Selena. I'll see you at the lawyer's office at 10 a.m. on Friday," Lena said before she got up and walked away.

"So, how did it go?" Alex asked when Lena got back in the car. He'd insisted on coming with her, but had grudgingly agreed to wait outside.

"She took it, just like I knew she would. There was no way her greedy ass would wait for me to get cash instead. As soon as she cashes it, I'll have more evidence of her blackmail scheme."

"That's good, I guess. Now, when are you going to tell your husband so this whole mess can go away?"

"He wants to go away on a honeymoon, so I guess I'll tell him after I have a few more days of wedded bliss."

"Is it really bliss with all of this crap hanging over your head?"

"It's as close to bliss as I think I'll get, so I'm going to enjoy it while I can."

"I really think you're selling Jonah short. I can't believe he'd leave you over this. He loves you, and has for years. I think he'll be mad, probably furious, but eventually he'll understand why you did what you did. One thing's for sure though, he won't be happy about how long it's taken you to come clean about it."

"You don't seem to understand, Alex. I'm never allowed to be happy for long. It's been that way my whole life. I know he'll leave me. That's just the way my life goes. Will you just let me enjoy it while I can? Please?"

Chapter 42

"So, Mrs. Parker, how was your day," Jonah asked when Lena walked in the door.

"It was productive, Mr. Parker," Lena said, smiling. "I got more done today than expected. In fact, after a meeting on Friday morning, I've cleared my calendar for the next three weeks."

"Really?"

"Yes. Sue agreed to stand in for me at the Foundation, no questions asked."

"That's great news. I've got things under control too. Does this mean we can sneak off for a honeymoon?"

"I don't see why not, Mr. Parker."

"Mrs. Parker, you make me such a happy man!"

"Are we ever going to get tired of referring to ourselves this way?"

"Sure. Soon, we'll be just like every other old married couple and the novelty will wear off."

"I hope not. I want it to feel like this forever."

"I think that can be arranged. Now, where do you want to go for our honeymoon?"

"Would you be disappointed if I said I wanted to stay right here?"

"You don't want to go to Miami, or Jamaica or Cancun or some trendy honeymoon spot?"

"No, I'd like to stay here and hide from the world. I'll go to the grocery store and buy everything we need for the next few weeks, then we won't even have to deal with delivery people."

"Okay, if that's what you really want."

"It is. I love it here and having you here with me makes it just about perfect. I'll do the shopping after my meeting, and we'll start our official honeymoon Friday evening. How's that sound?"

***

Friday morning, Lena arrived at Aaron Banks' office before ten, as planned. The lawyer had everything ready and waiting for her. "Thank you again for helping me with this, Aaron. I don't know what I would've done without you."

"I'm not exactly comfortable with what you're doing, Lena, but I'll go along with it for now. You will have to bring the police into it before the 30-day deadline we're giving your mother, or I'll be forced to go ahead and file the transfer paperwork."

"I understand. I've already talked to someone at the Sheriff's office and they agreed to work with you. I just need to let them know what's going on after we meet with Selena today."

"Good."

A knock on the door interrupted them, and a secretary ushered Selena into the office. She came through the door looking like death warmed over. She was skeletal thin and pale — the poster child for addiction.

I could almost feel sorry for her, if she wasn't trying so hard to ruin my life, Lena thought.

"Come in, Selena," Mr. Banks said, acting quite friendly. "I have everything ready to go. I'll just need to call Deborah and Carl from across the hall to come in and witness and notarize it once you've both signed.

"That paper means I own my house, right?"

"You will, once all the signatures are in place and I get it filed with the county. Thirty days from today, you'll be the proud new owner."

"Thirty days?"

"Why yes, it takes that long for the paperwork to make its way through the county's system once it's filed. I'll set up a meeting with you to come in and get the keys and final paperwork once everything is official."

"But I wanted to move in today!"

"I'm afraid that's not possible. Until the paperwork has been filed and accepted by the county, the property isn't actually yours."

"This is bull shit! You better not be tryin' ta trick me. I'll have your license if you are!"

"Ms. Walker, I assure you this is how things must be done if you want to have legal ownership of the property."

"Fine, but you better not be lyin' ta me."

"I am not."

"Okay, then. Let's get this show on the road. I don't wanna wait no longer than I have to. Already waited long enough as it is."

Once everyone had signed, the notary stamped, signed and dated the paperwork. "Thank you, Deborah and Carl. That's all we need from you for now."

"When will I get the deed and keys?"

"As I told you, once I receive word from the county that everything is filed and accepted, I'll contact you and set up an appointment so you can come and get them."

"She has ta have all her stuff out by then, right?"

"Yes, Lena has agreed to your demands and will remove her belongings once everything is official."

"Good. Like I said, can't happen fast enough. That house was always 'posed to be mine," Selena said, as she walked out the door and slammed it shut on her last word.

"She's a piece of work," Mr. Banks said.

"Yeah, she's something all right. I just won't say what in polite company."

Mr. Banks chuckled. "I understand perfectly. So, I'll be hearing from you before the 30-day mark?"

"Yes, I'll take care of things in the next few weeks and will let you know when to set the next meeting."

"I wish you luck, Lena. I hope we can put this mess behind us very soon."

Less than thirty days, Lena thought as she left the law office, *that may be all the time I get with Jonah. Why does that greedy bitch have to try to steal my happiness?*

Chapter 43

After five trips to the car, Lena had finally carried in all of the groceries she'd bought. *I think I got a little carried away, but I want the next few weeks to be as perfect as they can be, because this time might be all I get.*

She got busy putting things away, and heard the front door open and close a short time later. "Mrs. Parker, are you home?" Jonah called out as he walked through the house.

"I'm in the kitchen."

"Whoa! Did you buy out every store in town? Exactly how long are we going to be hiding out here?"

"I was hoping we could get in at least three weeks, maybe a little longer. What do you think?"

"If I had my way, we'd stay here forever and never have to deal with the outside world again."

"I feel the same way. Too bad the rest of the world won't cooperate."

"Yeah. I'd be surprised if we make it that long before people start hounding us."

"Well, we'd better make the most of every second of alone time we get then. Don't you think?"

"I do, and I'm going to help you put all of this stuff away so that we can get to some honeymoon action."

"Mr. Parker, are you suggesting we have a little afternoon delight?"

"Why yes, Mrs. Parker, that's exactly what I'm suggesting."

A short time later, Lena went into the bedroom with Jonah following close behind. He closed the bedroom door, and in one quick motion, pushed her against the wall and pressed himself against her. His lips kissed a trail down her neck, moving toward her breasts. His hands were at the back of her skirt, and it was unfastened and on the floor in seconds. The feel of it as it slid down to the floor gave Lena a tingling thrill.

His fingers tugged at her panties as his lips found her breasts. She made sure her panties hit the floor next, but Jonah didn't take the hint and switched his attention to the buttons on her blouse. Soon, it was removed as quickly as her skirt. Then, he stopped touching her and stood a fraction of an inch away, staring into her eyes. The sudden lack of sensation caused a shocked little sound of protest to escape from her lips.

That was all he needed. With only the slightest hint of a wolfish smile, he pushed himself against her and crushed her lips with another smoldering kiss.

He trailed kisses across her breasts, careful not to get too close to her needy nipples. It was torture. She wanted him to touch them. She wanted him to plunge his hand into her sex. *If he doesn't do something soon, I might scream!*

Lena let out a little pleading moan and pushed herself against him. He wouldn't have it though, and backed up slightly. He stopped touching her again to get his point across — he was in control.

Disappointed, she leaned back against the wall and waited. He returned her gaze with the same hungry animal look he'd worn earlier. It was intense and a huge turn-on.

This time when he embraced her, she could feel his need. He took her breath away when he cupped her sex in his hand and inserted three fingers slowly.

He knelt, then, and buried his face in her wet pussy. "Ahhh …" escaped her lips, but she said nothing else and tried not to move as he devoured her. This was what her body had been crying out for and she wanted to make sure he didn't stop.

He spread her swollen pussy lips with his hand, finding her clit and sucking at it eagerly. His efforts were rewarded by more tiny sounds. *She's going to cum if I keep this up,* Jonah thought, *and I don't want that. When she cums, it's going to be all over my dick, not my face!*

He stopped and stood to look at the effects he'd had on his new wife. Her face and breasts were flushed and her lips were slightly swollen and parted in anticipation. She was staring right back at him, her eyes greedily taking in the large bulge in his pants.

He slowly unfastened his belt and pants and pulled them and his briefs off, revealing his huge member was standing at attention. He could tell she wanted him to speed things up, but that wasn't what he had in mind. He was no horny schoolboy, she was his wife and he wanted to worship her body.

He grabbed her arm and spun her around, making her bend deep at the waist. He gave her ass a quick slap with his other hand and noted her legs were still spread wide. Taking advantage of this, he rammed his cock home in one smooth thrust. He was rewarded with a low moan from his partner and a hot, wet pussy clamped around his dick.

He grabbed the hair at the back of her head and wrapped his fist in it, pulling her head back and causing her back to arch and her ass to lift nicely. He grabbed her around the waist with his other arm and started pounding her pussy as hard as he could. Neither of them would last long like this. He could already feel her tightening and spasming around his dick.

He pulled her hair harder, adding pain to the pleasure and making her whimper. The sound just made him renew his efforts, ramming himself home harder and faster. He could feel the cum boiling up from his balls, but he didn't want to lose it yet, so he stopped.

Lena wanted to cry when he stopped. *I was so close!*

He held her there, motionless, for a full 10 seconds before he had himself under control enough to start banging away at her again. This time he rammed his cock in and then drew it out slowly, over and over until he knew he couldn't last much longer. He let go of her hair and grabbed both sides of her luscious ass for a better grip.

His efforts were anything but slow now. He drove his dick into her faster than he thought was possible, his balls tickling her clit he was so far in. He'd lost all control now and was making a low growling sound as he drove himself faster and faster as his climax neared.

Lena had never felt like this. The mix of pleasure bordering on pain had her frantic. She wanted to cum, she wanted to ram herself against him and rub her clit on whatever she could, but she didn't move and let him control her willingly.

His last thrust was deep and he kept it there for a few seconds until he felt the cum making its way to the head of his dick, then he pulled it from her sopping wet pussy so he could "decorate" her ass.

When his dick left her, she couldn't believe it. *I need to cum! What is he doing?*

With a grunt, he began spraying her ass with hot cum. He shot an amazing amount of the stuff, then rammed his dick home one more time.

That unexpected thrust sent Lena into orgasmic spasms. Her body shook with their intensity and the muscles in her pussy clenched the invading dick and covered it in her juices.

Neither of them spoke. There was no sound other than their panting. He gripped her ass for a few more seconds, relishing the moment, then released her.

"Wow! That was something," Lena panted as she used the dresser to steady herself. "You're an animal, Mr. Parker."

"Sorry about that, I got a little carried away."

"Don't be sorry. That was amazing!"

"I shouldn't be so rough with you. You're pregnant."

"I'm pregnant, not breakable, and I'm horny *all* the time now. That was just what the doctor ordered."

"Still, I'll try to keep it under control from now on."

"Not if I have anything to say about it, you won't," Lena said, laughing. "Now, how about a quick shower with me, so we can clean up a little and then do that again?"

"You have a definite naughty streak, Mrs. Parker. I think I like it."

***

In what seemed like the blink of an eye, three blissful weeks had gone by and Lena realized she was going to have to bite the bullet and tell Jonah her secret before time ran out. *I've never been this happy before, but I've also never dreaded anything more in my life than having to tell Jonah and wipe all this happiness away,* she thought as she drifted lazily around in her backyard pool. *I have to do it, though. It would be so much worse if he found out some other way. I know at some point Selena will find a way to tell him if I don't.*

She swiped furiously at the tears running down her face as she heard Jonah coming out onto the patio, and then dunked herself in the water to hide them from him.

"I hope you brought some lemonade with you," she said, forcing a smile. "This baby of yours can's seem to get enough of it."

"Oh, I've noticed, and I came prepared. I brought the whole pitcher."

"You're so smart and thoughtful. How did I get so lucky?"

"I'm the lucky one."

Yeah, you might not think that once I tell you everything, Lena thought morosely. *God, I hate this!* "Hey, how about I make a special dinner for us tonight?"

"You don't have to do that. We're supposed to be taking it easy, remember?"

"I want to. It's not going to be too complicated — I've got some nice steaks and the stuff to make a big salad. I might even make something fun for dessert."

"I know what I want for dessert..."

"You're insatiable! I meant something sweet—"

"So did I!"

"All right, you oversexed goofball, give me that lemonade and then I'm headed to the kitchen."

"Oooh, I've got every caveman's dream — my little barefoot and pregnant woman's gonna cook for me."

"Very funny. You'd better watch out or you won't get any of that sweet dessert you're hopin' for."

"Okay, okay, I'll be good."

Lena got out of the pool and gave Jonah a lingering kiss. She poured a glass of lemonade for him, then took the pitcher and headed to the kitchen."

"You're taking the whole pitcher?"

"I told you, your baby wants lemonade," she said, laughing as she went inside.

Chapter 44

"That was a great dinner, Mrs. Parker. Do you have anything in mind as an encore?"

"I do, but I'm afraid it's not what you're hoping for."

"What is it then? I suspect it can't be anything good, judging by the look on your face."

"I'm sorry to have to ruin what has been a perfect honeymoon, but I don't have a choice."

"Well, that sounds dire."

"Yeah, it kinda is. Why don't we go sit somewhere more comfortable before I begin?"

"You're stalling."

"I know, but I'm afraid nothing will be the same after I tell you what I have to tell you. These last few weeks, I've been happier than I can ever remember and I really don't want to give that up."

"Just tell me. I think doing it quickly, like ripping off a Band-Aid, is better than my imagination running wild."

"Yeah, I doubt you would ever imagine this," Lena muttered as she walked into the living room and sat down in a wing backed chair, while Jonah made himself comfortable on the couch next to her.

"Okay, remember when I told you that I tried to contact you multiple times back when we were teens."

"When that bitch Nicole lied to you and never told me? Yeah, I remember. Why?"

"You never asked why I was so desperate to talk to you. It wasn't just me being clingy or trying to stalk you. I truly needed to talk to you. When I thought you were ignoring me on purpose, I just assumed you wanted nothing more to do with me, but I had to try one more time. That's why I got your address and sent you that last letter."

"But I never got it."

"I know that now, but back then I thought you'd received it and read it because the post office didn't return it. I had no idea Nicole had taken it and you never saw it. Anyway, because I thought you'd read it and that you didn't care about what I'd told you, I made a huge decision."

"Okay, now you're scaring me. What decision? What exactly did that letter say?"

Lena didn't answer right away, she just stared at the floor, tears running down her face.

"What did it say, Lena?"

"I told you I was pregnant," Lena sobbed. "I begged you to contact me because I didn't know what to do."

"*What?*"

"I was pregnant. It was your baby. You know you were my first, and we didn't use protection that night."

"Oh, God—"

"Once I figured it out, I did everything I could to hide it from Selena. I did everything I could to keep her from finding out until I could move out and go to college. I thought I'd done it, too."

"Did you get an abortion?"

"No! That's what I'm trying to tell you. I hid the fact that I was pregnant. So, when I got to school, I started researching how private adoptions worked.

"I asked Mr. Banks, Gram's attorney, to help me. He was the only lawyer I knew and I was pretty sure I could trust him. He helped me find a couple who wanted a baby badly but couldn't have one of their own. They were perfect."

"How could you do that without involving me? Shouldn't I have had some say in the matter?"

"Mr. Banks knew I'd already tried repeatedly to contact you, and then he tried too — but he went through Nicole too, because that was the only way we thought we could contact you at that time. When there was no response from you on multiple occasions, he considered you were 'out of the picture,' and because of that the adoption could move forward without you."

"That doesn't seem right," Jonah muttered.

"At that time, it was the only way to proceed. I had to find a way for my baby to have a bright future with people who could love her and take care of her better than I could.

"I only got to hold her for a few minutes right after she was born because I had given the adoptive parents authorization to make her medical decisions and permission to take her home from the hospital as soon as she was released. It was easier for me if I didn't see her again, so I didn't get attached. After that, Mr. Banks filed a petition for adoption with the state of Georgia and she was officially theirs."

"So, I already have a kid out there somewhere? Do you know where she is?"

"Yes, but I'm not going to tell you."

"Why the fuck not? I think I have a right to know!"

"Actually, you don't. I know it's not your fault and it wasn't your choice, but because of what Nicole did, you ended up with no rights or say in the matter."

"*The matter?* Lena, this is my daughter we're talking about!"

"I know, but I'm not going to let you interfere in her life at this point. She's happy, healthy and her adoptive parents are wonderful. You meddling in her life because you feel you have a right to know her is not in her best interest and I'm not going to let you do that. I made a terrible sacrifice and gave her up so I could protect her and make sure she'd have the best life possible. I will *not* let you disrupt her life just because you have the emotional need to know a daughter you just found out about."

"I can't believe you're saying that." I have a *right* to know about my own flesh and blood!"

"No, you don't. Legally, you don't have any rights at all, and morally you should be more concerned about the damage you'd be doing to her — not your own selfish needs."

"Selfish? You're a fine one to talk about being selfish. Why didn't you tell me this sooner?"

"I actually hadn't planned to tell you at all, because I was afraid you'd react like this. Even though she's no longer mine, I will always protect her — even from you."

"If you weren't going to tell me, what changed? Why did you suddenly decide to come clean?"

"Selena is blackmailing me. She threatened to tell you if I didn't give her this house, because she thinks it should be hers, and also pay her $10,000 a month."

"So, you told me so you can keep the house and your money, but you wouldn't have otherwise? … I guess my first impression of you, when I didn't know who you were, was right. You're a *horrible* person," Jonah said, as he stood and stalked toward the door.

"Where are you going?"

"Away from you! I can't be around you anymore. I need time to think," he said as he grabbed his keys and walked out the door, slamming it behind him.

Lena ran to the door, but by the time she opened it and started outside, Jonah was already roaring out the driveway, tires screeching.

She came back inside and slowly closed the door, before putting her back against it and sliding to the floor, sobbing.

Chapter 45

Lena sat there crying, ignoring the discomfort of sitting on the entryway tile, until there were no more tears and she was exhausted. She struggled to get up, her pregnant belly getting in the way, and then stiffly walked to the bedroom she and Jonah had shared.

"Well, baby, I guess it's just you and me," she said, slowly running her hands over her stomach, before laying down on the bed and pulling up the sheet. "Mommy will make sure you're healthy, happy and well cared for.

The next morning, Lena felt horrible. Her head hurt from crying so much and the baby was restless; she could tell her mother was upset. "It's okay, baby. I'll be fine. I'm used to doing things by myself, so don't you worry. We've got an appointment with the doctor today, and I'm going to find out whether you're a boy or a girl. Won't that be fun?"

Thinking about the appointment brought on a whole new round of tears. *Jonah was supposed to be there today so we could find out together. I guess there won't be anymore together moments for us now,* she thought sadly as she prepared to shower and get ready to leave for the appointment.

Somehow, she managed to make it to the to the doctor's and through the ultrasound without crying, until she found out the sex of her baby. "Well, Mrs. Parker, it looks like you're going to have a little girl," the tech said happily, as Lena looked at the screen.

"She's beautiful," Lena said, and finally allowed the tears to come again.

"Would you like a copy of the image to take home with you?" the technician asked.

"Yes, that would be wonderful," Lena blubbered. "I'm sorry. I just can't seem to quit crying.

"Pregnancy hormones will get you every time," the tech said, chuckling as she clicked to capture the image.

"I think I need to come up with a name for you. Don't you?" Lena asked, as she sat in her car after the appointment, running her hands over her pregnant belly. "What do you think about combining Mommy and Daddy's name to make yours? How about Jolena? Let's try that out and see if we like it.

"Now, let's get you something to eat and call the sheriff's office to make sure our plan comes off without a hitch."

Chapter 46

The next few days felt like an eternity. Lena wandered around her house, feeling lost and completely alone — except for her unborn daughter. Bouts of crying that led to anger and ended at sorrow-filled acceptance cycled endlessly, so that by the end of each day she fell into bed, exhausted.

When Thursday, D-day, finally rolled around, she was filled with mixed emotions. For the hundredth time, she wondered, *How could Selena do this to me and threaten the happiness of the granddaughter she's never met? Oh God, please don't let me turn into her. Jolena deserves a mother who loves and protects her, not someone who will sell her out for profit. Today is going to be horrible, but satisfying. At least I'll know she can't hurt my family while she's in jail, and maybe she'll get clean while she's there.*

The undercover officers had agreed to meet at Aaron Banks' office at 3:30 to get things set up, so Lena left her home at three to make sure she got there on time. Her hands were shaking as she gripped the steering wheel, and the trepidation increased with each block she drove. *I'll be so glad when this is over.*

Even though she arrived 10 minutes early, the officers were already there, discussing things with Mr. Banks as she came through his office's front door. "Lena, join us, please," Aaron said, as she closed the door behind her. "I'd like to introduce you to Officer Frank James and Detective Jenna Stanley, some of Atlanta's finest. They'll be acting as our witnesses today and will be present for the entire meeting."

"Nice to meet you both," Lena said, shaking hands with each of them. "What do you need from me?"

"Ms. Walker—" Officer James started.

"Actually, it's Mrs. Parker. I got married a few weeks ago."

Oh, that's right. We knew that. Mrs. Parker, it wouldn't hurt if you got her to incriminate herself further," Officer James said. "Ask her to explain how she got this idea, how she plans to receive the additional payments she's demanding, that sort of thing."

"Your recent marriage is part of the reason we acted so quickly on this," Detective Stanley added. "It changes things when someone tries to extort money from a celebrity. Our department didn't want to get dragged through the mud by the tabloids for not doing something about it right away."

"I didn't realize you knew we got married."

"We're the law, ma'am, we kinda know everything," Detective Stanley said with a wink. "Anyway, we'd like you to act just like you would if we weren't here. Be angry and hurt — in other words, let your emotions flow. You don't want her to think anything odd is going on. We don't want her to decide to leave before we get enough to charge her."

"Okay, I can do that," Lena said, sounding less than confident.

"You'll be fine," Aaron said. "I'll help keep things moving in the right direction. You won't be doing it alone."

At exactly 4 p.m. on the dot, Selena came in the law office and slammed the door closed. "May I help you?" Detective Stanley asked from behind the secretary's desk.

"Yeah. I got an appointment with that uppity lawyer and my daughter. They here?"

"Can I have your name, please?" Detective Stanley asked, still playing the good secretary.

"It's Selena Walker. Now go tell 'em I'm here so we can get this show on the road."

"Just a moment, ma'am. I'll be right back," she said as she walked to Aaron's door, opened it and said, "Mr. Banks, there's a Selena Walker here to see you."

"Yes, yes, go ahead and send her in Jenna. I'll need you and James to join us for a few moments, too."

"I'll let him know and I'll be right—"

"Helena Sky Walker, you'd better be here with my money!" Selena yelled, interrupting the detective and shoving her out of the way as she stormed into the office.

"Ms. Walker, there's no need to be rude," Aaron admonished. "We're here waiting for you."

"Let's get this over with. I want my money and that paper that says the house is mine," Selena said as she flopped down into the other chair that sat in front of Aaron's large mahogany desk.

"Now, Ms. Walker, I've explained this to you," Aaron began, "you'll be getting the final paperwork and keys to the house after you sign the final paperwork showing you've received them. Jenna and James will be the witnesses for that signature," he said, indicating the two people who had just entered his office.

"What's with all this official bullshit? You tryin' to scam me or somethin'?"

"Selena, as I told you before, the paperwork had to be recorded by the county, and now we need a signature from you showing you've received the paperwork and the keys. Once that's done, everything is official. You want it to be official, right?"

"Yeah. Why's everythin' gotta take so dang long?"

"You know anything involving the government takes a lot of paperwork and a long time, Selena. You're getting everything you want, so stop being such a bitch," Lena said quietly.

"Is that any way to talk to your momma?"

"Selena, you stopped being my momma a long time ago. Now, you're just some scam artist who's blackmailing me."

"That's harsh."

"Yeah, but it's true. What would you call threatening to go to the press and Jonah about things you know I don't want made public and then telling me you'll keep quiet if I give you my house and $10,000 a month? I'd call that blackmail."

"You owe me, girl. I'm only askin' for what's rightfully mine."

"Exactly how do you figure that, Selena? How do I owe you anything? The only thing you did was give birth to me, other than that you haven't been my mother at all."

"She had no right to leave my house to you! It's mine! She was s'posed to leave it to me — I'm her daughter."

"Gram raised me and I was more of a daughter to her than you ever were. You're the only one who thinks she owed you anything. You gave her nothing but grief your whole life."

"How did I give her grief?"

"Oh, let's see, all the men you paraded through her home, the drugs, stealing from her. Want me to go on?"

"Oh, shut up. You don't know what my life was like."

"Whatever, Selena. I just want to you stay away from me. I'll pay you, but you stay the hell out of my life or the money stops."

"The money stops and I go to the press and your precious man."

"Jonah already knows, so that threat won't work with me anymore, but I don't want you dragging his name into this so the tabloids can have a field day. That's the only reason I'm even dealing with you. I want to protect him."

"You always were a stupid little twat. Oh well, you bein' stupid is gonna buy me a lot of nice stuff."

"Ladies, I think we've gotten off track here," Aaron said. "Why don't we get this paperwork dealt with so you can be on your way?" Aaron shuffled the papers in front of him and said, "Ladies, I need your signatures in the places indicated by the tabs, so why don't we move over to the table in the corner?"

Aaron pointed to each line slowly, which made Selena's impatience come to a head. "Before we sign this damn paper, I want my money."

"Wow, you really are a greedy, awful person, aren't you?" Lena asked with contempt. "I've got your damned money right here in my bag. Have you already run through the first ten grand I gave you?"

"Well, a girl has ta shop and I have needs," Selena said petulantly. "I've done without for a lot of years because of you. You owe me."

"I'm not really sure how you going without has anything to do with me. You only took care of me for a few months when I was a teenager."

"Whatever. I got needs and you owe me, so give me my money."

"Fine," Lena growled, pulling the cashier's check from her bag. "Here's your blackmail money. Don't spend it all on drugs this time."

"This was supposed to be cash! You stupid or somethin', girl?"

"I told you before, the bank has rules about cash amounts that big."

"You're an idiot. Should'a got it out in smaller amounts. Whatever. I can make this work," Selena said as she grabbed the check, folded it and stuffed it in her bra.

"Well, that's classy," Lena said, shorting out a laugh. "Maybe you can use some of that money to buy a wallet so you don't have to use your bra as a purse."

"Yeah, I ain't fancy like you—"

"Ladies, can we get back to the document, please? I have another appointment in 20 minutes, so we need to wrap this up."

"Great. Hurry this up, then. I ain't got all day neither. I got things ta do."

"Mr. Banks, I forgot to give you this form," Jenna said, handing him a piece of paper.

"What's that?" Selena asked. "More damn papers for me to sign?"

"Actually, yes," Aaron said. "This is a bit of protection for Lena. It lays out the deal between the two of you, about the house and the monthly payments and states that by giving you those things she's buying your silence. You'll need to sign it and I'll keep it on file."

"Okay, whatever. Hand it over."

Everyone watched as Selena signed what was basically her confession to extort money and property from her daughter. *I can't believe she fell for that. Greed will get you every time,* Lena thought.

When she finished signing, Selena started to hand the paper to Aaron. "Oh, would you please give that to Jenna? She'll be the one filing it."

"Sure, here you go."

"Thank you, Ms. Walker," Jenna said with a smile. "You're under arrest. You have the right to remain silent—"

"Under arrest? What're you playin' at, girl?"

"Ms. Walker, I'm Detective Jenna Stanley, and that guy over there is Officer Frank James," Jenna said, pulling her badge from her pocket. "You're being charged with theft by extortion under Georgia Code 16-8-16, and we were both witnesses to you admitting to doing what we're charging you with. We also have your signed confession right here," she said, waving the paper Selena had just signed.

Aaron smiled. "I told you what this paper said, and you willingly signed it and handed to the detective. There are multiple witnesses to what just occurred."

"*You set me up?*" Selena screeched.

"Did you really think I was going to give you Gram's house and all that money?" Lena asked.

"But you gave me ten grand. I spent it. You can't get it back, ya dumb bitch."

"That was a small price to pay to get you out of my life for up to ten years."

"Ten years? I didn't even do nothin'. How can I go away for ten years?"

"Ma'am, that's the maximum time a judge could give you for extortion here in Georgia," Officer James said. "So, it's very possible your sentence could be that long."

"Helena Sky Walker, I'm your mother! How could you do this to me?"

"Same way you could blackmail your daughter."

"I don't wanna go to jail!" Selena wailed. "I didn't do nothin'! You *owed* me."

"Selena, I don't owe you anything," Lena said, standing to leave. "Officer, Detective, do you need anything else from me? I've had about all of this I can take."

"We'll need a statement from you," the detective said, "but you can come down to the station tomorrow and do that if you want."

"Thank you all for your help with this matter," Lena said, shaking hands with each of them in turn. "You don't know how relieved I am that this ordeal is finally over."

As Lena walked out the front door of the law office, she heard the detective ask, "Ms. Walker are you going to go peacefully or do I have to cuff you?"

***

Chapter 47

I don't know why I don't feel more relieved that she's out of my life, Lena thought as she pulled into her driveway. She's never cared about me and I always knew that, but it still hurts to see it firsthand. This whole thing just makes me feel so sad.

As she started up the walk to the back door, she was startled to see someone sitting on the steps. "Can I help you?" she asked, keeping her distance until the person turned toward her and she saw it was Alex.

"Alex! What are you doing here?"

"Well, I thought I'd better check on my best friend, since she's supposed to be on her honeymoon but her husband has been spotted running around Hollywood all by himself."

"So that's where he went. I thought he was going to the new house. Guess that was too close to me for comfort."

"What are you talking about?"

"He stormed out of the house after I told him everything. That was about a week ago and I haven't heard from him since. I'm pretty sure he's not coming back, Alex."

"Wow, I'm sorry. You should've called me. ... Listen, I'm sure he just needs some space. He'll come back when he's got his head on straight."

"I hope you're right. Why don't you come in? My back and feet are killing me and I really need to sit down. We'll get comfortable and I'll tell you all about it."

Alex sat in Lena's living room, wearing a shocked look on his face after she told him how Jonah had reacted to her news.

"I can understand your reasoning for not telling him," Alex said, "but I can also understand where Jonah's coming from. He just found out he has a kid. That has to be a huge shock."

"I know, and I feel horrible about having to tell him the way I did. I think part of the reason he's so furious with me is because I told him if it wasn't for her threats I might not have ever told him."

"Well, you did agree to no more secrets, and he trusted you to mean it."

"I know, but that secret wasn't really mine to tell anymore. It involves other people whose lives could possibly be ruined if it gets out."

"Maybe, once he's had a chance to cool off and think things through, he'll understand."

"I doubt it. He won't even speak to me, and apparently, he can't even stand to be in the same state. Enough about my miserable life, I want to know about you and Sue. Give me the juicy details so I can think about something happy for a while."

"Are you sure? I'm worried about you and—"

"I'm sure. I want to hear some good news for a change."

"It *is* good. Sue and I are going to try having a relationship."

"That's great! I'm sorry if I hurt your feelings with the whole date-switching thing," Lena said, smiling, "but I'm kinda glad I did."

"I am too. You're a bit of a bitch sometimes, you know that?" Alex asked, laughing. "But I forgive you, because I know you did it with good intentions. Sue and I are in a really good place, and I think maybe it might turn into something more than just mind-blowing sex. So, thanks for meddling."

"I'm so happy for the two of you. Try not to screw it up like I did. Okay?"

***

Chapter 48

Weeks went by, and Lena buried herself in her work to keep her mind off her broken heart. The Foundation had rebounded nicely and everyone seemed to have forgotten the scandal surrounding it. Working with Jonah had opened doors to other celebrities and several had agreed to donate their time and talents to help with fund-raising. The work was gratifying and Lena made sure she worked to the point of exhaustion each day so there was no time left to feel sorry for herself.

Worry was starting to creep in though. The final concert of Jonah's contract was only six weeks away, and she wondered if he would honor it. She'd been avoiding even thinking about it, but she was going to have to contact his people to make sure it was still going to happen. There'd be no reason to spend the time and money promoting it if he was going to cancel, so she decided to bite the bullet and contact Jonah's tour manager.

Lena pressed the intercom, "Victoria, can you get Jeff Johnson on the line for me, please."

"Who's Jeff Johnson?" Victoria asked in her usual petulant voice.

"Really, Victoria? Do you ever pay attention to anything that goes on around here? He's Jonah Parker's tour manager. He should be on the contact list."

Just as Lena was getting ready to go find the number herself, Victoria announced Jeff was on line one. *She probably knew who he was all along,* Lena thought. *I swear, I'm getting closer to dismissing her ass every day.*

"Jeff? Hi, it's Lena at the Good Samaritan's Foundation. How are you? I was just calling to make sure everything's on schedule for Jonah's concert at State Farm Arena."

"Yeah, everything's good on our end. Our people should be there next week to check things out. I'll be sure they connect with you while they're there."

"That's great, Jeff. I'll talk to you soon."

Well, that's a relief, Lena thought after hanging up. *Guess we'd better get busy promoting this thing.*

For the next six weeks, Lena worked tirelessly behind the scenes to make sure the concert would be a success. Her days were long, and she managed to keep her mind off Jonah most of the time. She was more driven than usual, but as far as anyone at work was concerned, she was just being her controlling self and no one thought twice about it.

The only time she allowed herself to wallow in self-pity and regret was during her ultrasound appointments. She'd intended to share those moments with Jonah, and his absence tore at her heart even as she experienced the joy of seeing her healthy baby girl on the screen.

She knew these sad moments were going to happen more often now that the doctor had set up appointments every three weeks. Jonah was going to miss them all.

***

Chapter 49

The day of the concert arrived, and Lena was on-site directing every last detail of the setup. She had vowed this concert was going to be perfect and refused to leave anything to chance, even though she was exhausted most of the time now.

"Come on, guys. This needs to be set up by three so they can start the sound checks. Move faster, please." *Yeah, you need to be done so I can get out of here before Jonah arrives. So, hurry up!*

The concert had been sold out for weeks, so there was no promotion left to do, no more planning, just seeing to these final details and then supervising the tear-down afterwards. *I'm glad this is almost over. I feel like I need to sleep for a week,* Lena thought as she hurried to check backstage to make sure the craft services people were setting up.

A short time later, she made a final walk-through to check every detail one more time. Things looked good, and there was no time to spare. *I've got to get out of here. I don't think I can deal with seeing Jonah right now, and I certainly don't want to jeopardize the concert by pissing him off right before he's supposed to perform.*

Lena left and headed to the Omni. She'd be hanging out there until the concert was over. Not being there to see all of the hard work come together was going to be tough, but it was for the best. She had confidence that her staff could handle anything that came up at this point. "I'm going to kick off my shoes, order room service and eat my weight in ice cream and cake. I think I deserve a treat," she said to herself as she walked to her hotel room.

Lena had asked Sue to call her when the concert was over, so she could come back and oversee the tear-down to make sure everything went off without a hitch. Having no personal life to speak of after Jonah walked out had caused her to focus all her energies on making everything she did perfect as possible. She thought it was probably driving her staff crazy, but it seemed like the only way she could feel in control of her life at the moment.

When she got the all-clear call from Sue and she walked back to the venue and got to work. Everything was going smoothly, and the crew doing the tear-down was almost finished when Lena suddenly felt strange. She started walking over to where Sue was supervising the people packing up Foundation banners and materials, to let her friend know she was going to take a break and sit down for a minute. "Hey, Sue," she called out while she was still several feet away, "I'm going to—"

Sue watched in horror as Lena crumpled to the floor. "Oh, my God. Lena, are you okay?" she cried as she ran over to her friend. "Lena? Hey, are you okay?" she asked as she lightly patted her friend's cheek. When she got no response, she yelled, "Someone call an ambulance — now!"

Sue and Alex followed the ambulance to nearby Emory University Hospital. Since they weren't related, they'd been shuttled to the ER waiting room where they sat tensely awaiting news. "I hope the baby's okay," Sue said, wringing her hands with worry."

"I'm sure everything will be fine," Alex said, stilling her hands and then holding them. "Lena's a fighter, and I'm positive her baby is too."

"You're right, I just wish I knew what was taking so long."

"You know how hospitals are, nothing ever happens quickly. But, if I know Lena, as soon as they tell her we're out here waiting, she'll have someone come and get us."

Two hours and several unsuccessful trips to the nurse's station to ask for status reports later, a doctor finally came out to talk to them. "Mrs. Parker is stable," the doctor said, watching as both of the people he was addressing visibly relaxed. "She's experiencing preeclampsia and I've given her an IV cocktail of drugs to lower her blood pressure. Right now, it looks like that's working. We're going to admit her and monitor her and the baby. The goal is to get her to at least 37 weeks, but we might have to induce her before that to keep mother and baby both healthy."

"Oh, my God, this is serious. Alex, you need to track down Jonah and let him know right away."

"I can try, but I know Jonah. When he's made a decision to shut someone out, he does it. I'll make some calls and see what I can find out."

"Do what you have to do. None of us would be able to forgive ourselves if something happened and he wasn't here. Lena, shouldn't have to go through this by herself.

Sue turned toward the doctor, who had stepped back to give them some privacy, and asked hopefully, "Can we see her now, doctor?"

"Are you related?"

"No, we're her best friends."

"Let me check with the patient and if she says it's okay, then I'll send a nurse to take you to her."

***

Chapter 50

L ena spent the next three weeks in the hospital, being mon-
itored constantly. Sue and Alex took turns sitting with her
and keeping her up to date on everything going on in the
outside world.

"I'm losing my mind," Lena complained for the millionth
time. "I'm so bored that I actually look forward to the times
when they let me walk the halls."

"We know, sweetie, but you're doing this for a good reason,"
Sue said. "That baby needs to stay in there as long as possible."

"I know, I know. … It's just torture being here and doing
nothing all day long every day."

"I wouldn't say you've done nothing. You've come up with
several interesting new projects for the Foundation while you've
been trapped here."

"Yeah, but I can't do anything to get them started. I hate feeling useless."

"Your job right now is to grow that baby, and nothing else.
So, quit your whining," Sue said, pointing her finger at Lena and
laughing.

"Still no word from Jonah?" Lena asked, sounding forlorn and miserable.

"I'm afraid not. Alex says he's looked everywhere for him — all his usual hideouts — but he hasn't spoken to him."

"Figures. Only *I* could make the man I love run to the ends of the earth to get away from me. I wish I'd told him sooner. I just want it to be our daughter's choice to know us. Is that so bad?"

"I understand why you did what you did, honey, but men don't think that way. I really hope that once he has some time to cool off and think about it, he'll understand. I'm not so sure he'll ever understand why you took so long to tell him, though."

"I know," Lena moaned. "I've been beating myself up about that the whole time I've been stuck here. I can't change what I've done, but it doesn't seem to stop me from playing it over and over in my head."

"You need to stop torturing yourself. The ball's in his court. He'll either forgive you or he won't. The thing is, you have a new life growing inside you and she needs all of your love and attention right now. Think about her and all of the things the two of you will do together as she grows up. Those are much better thoughts to have swirling around in that busy head of yours."

"Thanks for being here, Sue. You're always able to talk sense into me. I'm so glad we're friends — and that you're so damn persistent."

"For you, always! Now, let's get ready, *The Bachelor* is about to come on and we need to see who's gonna get that rose."

"Ugh, I can't believe you like that show."

Chapter 51

Two more weeks dragged by, and Lena got progressively more grouchy as the days wore on. "Alex, you realize this hospital stay is costing me a fortune. Right?"

"Quit complaining. You can afford it."

"I know, but I spent so many years watching every penny and this just seems extreme."

"It is, but it's worth it for what you're getting."

"What, more annoyed by the day?"

"No, a healthy baby who's spent enough time developing that she hopefully won't have complications."

"I know. I'm just being bitchy. It doesn't help that I know we're into the safe zone at 35 weeks. I love this baby with everything I've got, but I really want her out of me!"

"I know!" Alex said, laughing. "You tell us that every day. Just remember, every extra day she's inside you is a gift."

"Yeah, yeah, yeah. Quit being such a Pollyanna. I want to be grumpy."

"Well, you're doing a great job!"

"Oh, shut up and get the cards. Maybe a game will help get my mind off how uncomfortable I am."

Three hours and many card games later, Alex put the deck away and prepared to leave. "It's time for a changing of the guard," he announced as Sue walked through the door. "You'd better watch out, honey, the prego is in a mood today."

"Oh really?" Sue asked, smiling. "How is that any different from yesterday and the day before?"

"Well, I think she's ramped it up a notch."

"Oh, God," Sue said in mock horror.

"Cut it out, you guys," Lena said, acting hurt by their teasing. "You know how much I appreciate you being here. I would've truly lost my mind if not for you. I just can't help being a grouch. I'm fat and uncomfortable and trapped here where no one will let me do anything except go to the bathroom and walk the halls, and I have to have a chaperone when I do either thing."

"Enjoy the rest and quiet now, 'cause when that baby gets here, that's all going to go away."

"I know, and I can't wait. At least after she's born, I'll have something meaningful to do and they'll *let me go home!*"

"Oh, here we go again," Alex said, grinning. "I think that's my cue to leave. I'll see you later, grouchy-pants, and I'll see you tonight. Right, Sue?"

"You couldn't keep me away."

"Aww, you guys are so cute that I could just puke."

"See what I mean?" Alex asked as he headed out the door.

"Well, Miss Thing, I can tell I'm in for a rough evening. What's got your panties in a bunch?"

"I am *so* sick of being here! Plus, there's not one position I can find where I'm comfortable *and* I feel like a beached whale."

"Well, let's see if we can't find something to take your mind off that for a little while," Sue said as she flipped through the TV channels.

A few hours later, Sue got ready to take her leave as visiting hours came to an end. She'd managed to keep Lena occupied most of the evening.

"Sue, thank you for putting up with me. I was in a pretty bad place mentally today."

"No problem. You just owe me big time once that baby's born."

"Okay. I'll be happy to do whatever horrendous things you come up with to pay you back."

Sue laughed, then said her goodbyes and headed to Alex's place.

Once Lena was alone, she felt herself slipping back toward depression. *I have got to snap out of this,* she thought. *All of this sadness and feeling sorry for myself can't be good for Jolena. Maybe I can find a funny movie to watch until I can fall asleep.*

Lena woke suddenly at 2 a.m. with a sharp pain in her abdomen. It was so severe she couldn't move. "Something's wrong," she gritted out, trying to reach the call button to summon the nurse. When she finally grasped it, she pressed the button repeatedly, desperate to summon help. *Oh, God, I can't be losing you, Jolena. Hold on, baby, someone will be here to help any minute,* she thought as she fought through another wave of pain.

A few minutes later, a nurse hurried into the room. "What seems to be the problem, Mrs. Parker?"

"Pain," Lena grunted out. "So bad … can't move."

"Oh, my. Your blood pressure is way up. I'll call the doctor right away," she said as she nearly ran from the room.

An excruciating thirty minutes later, Lena's doctor arrived and started evaluating her. "I suspect it's a rare disorder called HELLP syndrome. It's kind of like a more severe form of preeclampsia, Mrs. Parker. If I'm right, I think you're going to meet your daughter very soon. We're going to check your liver enzymes and platelet levels and find out for sure. For now, I'm going to increase your anti-hypertensive medication and get your blood pressure lowered, and I'll also give you a low dose pain reliever.

"The good news is, once you've delivered your daughter, your health should start improving almost immediately."

"Is my baby okay?" Lena asked, cradling her stomach and rubbing it in an effort to calm the pain.

"We're watching her vitals carefully, and so far, she's not in any danger," the doctor said reassuringly. "I'm going to go try to speed up those test results. If I'm right, we'll need to get you prepped for an emergency C-section."

"Can someone call my friends and let them know what's happening? They're on my emergency contact list. I need them here."

"Sure. I'll ask a nurse to do that for you right away, and someone will be in to adjust your meds soon. Don't worry, we're going to take good care of you."

Once the medication started kicking in, the pain let up a little and Lena fell into a troubled sleep. Her mind was working overtime to create nightmares filled with all sorts of horrible things, mostly involving the loss of her precious Jolena.

She woke with a start to find Alex and Sue standing by her bedside. "Hey, Sleeping Beauty," Alex said softly, "how're you doing?"

"Better," Lena said, groggily. "Doesn't hurt so much right now."

"We talked to your doctor," Sue said. "They're preparing to do an emergency C-section. Apparently, your test results weren't good, so you're going to meet your daughter sooner than expected."

"No-o-o-o! She can't come when Jonah's not here. He needs to be here. She needs her daddy!" Lena wailed, and started to try to get up out of bed. "I have to go find him. He has to be here!"

"Calm down, honey," Alex said in a soothing voice. "You can't go anywhere. You're about to have a baby."

"You don't understand, Alex," Lena pleaded, sounding frantic, "he *has* to be here. *I want my husband, Alex!*"

"Okay, I understand," Alex said, trying to calm her. "How about I go find him and you stay right here?"

"I won't go anywhere, I promise. I'll stay right here in bed."

"Good. You need to be thinking about Jolie right now."

"Jolie?"

"That's the nickname her godparents have come up with for her."

"Oh, I like that! I'll be good, I promise. Now, please, go find my husband," Lena said, then laid her head back and closed her eyes.

"I'll leave right away. Don't you worry about a thing. Sue will stay here with you, but I need to talk to her before I leave."

"Sue, will you walk me out?" Alex asked quietly.

"Do you really think you can find Jonah and get him here?" Sue asked as soon as they stepped into the hall.

"I have a confession to make," Alex said, looking contrite. "I tracked him down two weeks ago, I just haven't been able to talk sense into him. I don't think he really understands what's going on because he's been too drunk to reason with. He's a stubborn ass when he wants to be."

"Well, you need to get him here — even if you have to tie him up and put him in your trunk. Reading between the lines of what the doctor told us, I think this is an extremely serious situation for both Lena and the baby. He needs to be here in case something happens. Hell, he should be here anyway — he's about to be a father!"

"I'll do my best. I just hope he hasn't taken off again."

Chapter 52

Alex left the hospital and headed straight for Jonah's Atlanta home. He felt bad about not telling Lena that Jonah was back in town, but he also knew his friend needed some time to come to terms with his hurt and anger.

He pulled up outside Jonah's house, got out and jogged to the front door. He rang the bell several times and stood there waiting impatiently. When he didn't hear anyone moving around inside, he started pounding on the door and shouting, "Come on, man. I know you're in there. Answer the damned door. It's an emergency!"

He continued pounding on the door, rattling it in its frame and growing more frustrated every second. "Jonah! Answer the damned door!" he yelled, as he continued to pound away. Suddenly, his fist met air as the door flew open.

"What the fuck do you want?" Jonah yelled. "Do you know what time it is?"

"I don't care what time it is," Alex said angrily. "You need to get dressed and come with me to the hospital. *Right now!*"

"What the hell are you talking about? Why do I need to go to the hospital at 4 a.m.? ... Wait, is it the baby?"

"You're an asshole. You know that, right?" Alex asked, disgusted. "Your wife and daughter are in critical condition, and there's a chance you could lose one or even both of them and you can't get past your hurt feelings to be there for them? You're not the man I thought you were," Alex said, looking defeated as he turned to go back to his car.

"Wait! What do you mean I could lose them? What's happened?"

"Like I've been trying to tell you for the last two weeks, Lena has not been well. She was hospitalized for a reason, you idiot. They were trying to let the baby get as far along as possible before they had to induce labor. Well, a few hours ago things got worse — a lot worse — and they're prepping her for an emergency C-section as we speak."

"I thought you were exaggerating and trying to guilt-trip me into forgiving her. You never really acted like it was that serious."

"I didn't want to scare you, stupid," Alex spat out. "Lena was terrified and stressed, and I didn't want you in the same shape. I wanted to give you time to cool down. I thought you would do the decent thing and go to see your pregnant wife. I guess I should have tried scaring the shit out of you instead, maybe that would have penetrated that thick skull of yours."

"I can't lose them, Alex," Jonah said, sounding like he was just about to cry. "I love Lena but I couldn't get past my anger and confusion. I was suffering, so I wanted her to suffer too — but not like this. I'd hate myself if something bad happened and I wasn't there for them."

"Okay, you idiot, let's go! It's time for you to stop fucking up and be there for them."

"Okay, let me throw on some clothes—"

"Shower first. You stink like whiskey!"

Alex got Jonah to the hospital in record time, and they came down the hall just as the orderlies were wheeling Lena to surgery. "Wait!" Jonah yelled to them as he started running down the hall. "Lena, I'm here!"

"Jonah," Lena said groggily. "Is that really you or am I imagining it again?"

"It's me," Jonah said as he came to stand beside her. "I was an idiot, and I'm sorry I stayed away so long."

"It's okay," Lena slurred, "you're here now and that's what matters. We're going to meet our daughter. I've named her Jolena. Did you know that? It's our two names crammed together," Lena said, giggling, obviously high from the preoperative meds.

"Sir, we need to get her to surgery," one of the orderlies said, as they started pushing her down the hall again.

"Bye-bye, Jo-Jo," Lena said in a goofy voice, as the orderlies pushed the gurney through the door to the surgery suite.

"Well, at least she saw you before the surgery," Alex said, "but I'm not sure she actually knows you're here. She was pretty drugged-up."

"Yeah, I don't think she's ever called me Jo-Jo before. That was weird." Turning serious, Jonah said, "Thanks for giving me the kick in the ass I needed to get me here. I'm not even sure why I was being so stubborn. I guess I was waiting for her to come crawling back to me, even though I knew deep down that she never would."

"No, she wouldn't have been able to do that. She's got a lot of childhood baggage that revolves around being unwanted, and she avoids meeting that possibility head-on whenever she can. She was sure you didn't want or love her anymore because of what she did, and she thought she was on her own again."

"I knew that about her, and I still couldn't get past my stupid hurt feelings. I even understand why she didn't tell me. I don't know, it was just easier to hold a grudge than to open myself up to more emotions. So, I hid and avoided it all."

"Well, it's time to stop hiding and start acting like an adult. You're about to become a father, *again,* and this time you have the chance to be there for your child. Don't blow it!"

"I hear you, loud and clear."

"You'd better," Sue said as she walked up to them, "'cause if you don't step up, you're gonna find my boot in your ass! I think you've more than made Lena pay for not telling you. You've been a five-star jackass to my best friend. She's been in the hospital for weeks and you didn't even bother to call and find out how she was doing. She's your wife. She shouldn't have gone through this alone!"

"I know I behaved like a jerk. You don't have to beat me up, I've been doing that enough for the both of us all the way here. I'm just glad she had you and Alex there with her."

"Maybe you can start to make up for things by finding out if you can be in there with her," Sue said pointedly. "I think it's the least you can do. I'm going to find some coffee. The doctor said it will be a while."

"Well, I guess she put you in your place. I can't say I wasn't expecting that," Alex said, wearing a small grin. "I think you'd better go find out about attending your daughter's birth or you might have to be admitted to the hospital so they can remove Sue's boot from your ass!"

"Agreed."

"The nurse's station is down the hall and to the left. Good luck. Sue and I will be waiting to hear all about how Miss Jolena Parker made her grand entrance to this world. Go get 'em, Daddy!"

Seventy-five tense minutes later, a nurse came into the waiting room to let Alex and Sue know that everything had gone well. "You two can see them in just a bit. We'll be moving Mrs. Parker back to her same room once the doctor okays it. You can go ahead and wait there if you want."

The couple thanked the nurse and went straight to Lena's room. "I can't wait to see the little girl who's caused all this fuss," Sue said, excitedly.

"I'm just glad they're both okay. Maybe we can all put this behind us and things can get back to normal."

"Yeah, that would be nice. I haven't been spending nearly enough time with my new boyfriend," Sue said.

"Don't I know it!" Alex said, laughing.

A short time later, the orderlies wheeled Lena back into the room, with Jonah following close behind. She was smiling from ear to ear. "You guys, she's beautiful!"

"With the two of you for parents, how could she be anything else?" Sue asked. "Where is she? We want to meet her."

"The nurse is supposed to bring her here as soon as they get her cleaned up."

***

Epilogue

hree weeks later, Lena was scrambling to get the baby and herself ready for the christening ceremony. "I'm so glad the pastor agreed to do the ceremony here," Lena said as Jonah came into the room. "It simpler, and it makes me feel like Gram is somehow a part of it because we're having it in her garden."

"I think she would have loved it," Jonah said, "but she would not approve of you attending in your pajamas. Do you plan to get dressed soon? You know my parents are always early to everything, and I'm pretty sure my other relatives will be early too."

"I know, I know. Jolena was being fussy this morning and it took longer than I thought to get her to eat."

"Well, you go get ready and I'll take care of our grumpy daughter. I hope she doesn't plan to scream through the whole ceremony."

"She's a little diva. I'm sure she'll realize she's the center of attention and be all smiles."

"I hope you're right, because it sure would make things easier."

Ten minutes before the ceremony was schedule to start, Sue went to check on Lena and make sure she was going to be ready soon. "Lena," she called as she knocked on the door to the master suite, "are you about ready? Everyone is here and they're wondering where you are."

"I'm in the bathroom," Lena said, sounding like she was about to burst into tears.

"What's wrong, honey?" Sue asked, coming into the bathroom.

"Nothing fits!" Lena wailed, pulling at her dress with unshed tears pooling in her eyes, as she moved back into the bedroom. "I've put on so much weight—"

"Stop right there. First, you just had a baby, and second, you are beautiful. It's a little tight, but we can fix it, don't cry. Do you have a pretty shawl? We can use it as camouflage and you'll look wonderful."

"I've got several in my closet," Lena said pitifully, "but I don't see how that's going to help."

"Let me see what you've got, and then I'll fix you right up," Sue said as she headed toward the closet.

A few minutes later, she appeared in the doorway holding a beautiful, delicate shawl. "Come here and let me work my magic," she said, as she gathered and twisted the material.

She helped Lena put it on, then made several adjustments before stepping back to admire her work. "I think that will do just fine."

"Really?"

"If you don't believe me, go look in the mirror."

Lena walked slowly over to the full-length mirror, then closed her eyes and moved to stand in front of it.

"You have to open your eyes or you won't know how fantastic you look," Sue said with a grin.

"I'm afraid to look," Lena said in a whiny voice.

"Open your eyes, you big baby!" Sue scolded.

"Oh, my God. Sue, you're a miracle worker. That looks amazing."

"Told you so. Now, come on. You've got a whole garden full of people waiting to see you."

"They're waiting to see you and Alex too. I'm so happy you guys agreed to be Jolena's godparents. There's no one in the world I trust more than the two of you."

"Oh, shut up. You're going to make me cry and ruin my makeup."

The christening went off without a hitch, and everyone went home happy after holding and fawning over the beautiful Jolena. Once the caterer's crew had cleaned everything up, the three of them finally found themselves alone.

"This is the life I've always wanted," Lena said, giving her husband a warm hug. "A family, friends, white picket fence, the whole nine yards. Everything that led up to this day was hard, but we survived it, and I wouldn't change anything. I think maybe we had to go through the fire and get to the other side so we would appreciate what we have. We have a beautiful child, a village to help raise her, and each other.

"I don't want to go through those rough times again, so I promise I'll never keep big secrets from you again."

"Only big secrets? What about the little ones?"

"A girl has to have some mystery, and it adds a little spice to the romance," Lena said, batting her eyelashes.

"I suppose she does, and I look forward to exploring every one of them with you for the rest of my life."

There was a loud knock at the door, interrupting their blissful embrace. "Wonder who that could be," Jonah said, with a little irritation.

"I don't know," Lena said, heading to answer the door. "Whoever it is, I'm going to get rid of them. I'm tired."

When Lena opened the door, an young girl stood there looking at her expectantly. "May I help you?"

"Yes, ma'am. I'm looking for Helena Sky Walker."

"You've found her. What can I do for you?"

"Well, I'm hoping you can answer some questions for me. ... You're my birth mother."

To be continued...

Thank you for reading! I hope you enjoyed the story and plan to read books two and three in the Everlasting Trilogy —

At Last, Yours & Eternally Mine!

Please enjoy this sneak peek of...

At Last, Yours

The door to the limousine opened and Alexander took an anxious breath. This was the night. He had finally told Lena how he felt, and now he would find out if she felt the same way. The minute he saw the color of the leg, shoes, and dress, he knew. He finally had his answer, and wasn't the one he wanted

"Surprised?" Ms. McKinley asked Alex after she seated herself in the limo and the driver closed the door.

"Mildly."

"You're not disappointed that I'm not Lena?"

Alex looked at the temptress with a mixture of confusion, curiosity, and desire. True, from the moment he first saw her, he thought she was one of the most beautiful women he'd ever seen. In fact, he'd froze like a deer in headlights when Lena made the introductions.

"I don't know what I feel."

"Well, I'm happy to continue with whatever plans you had for you and Lena, unless of course you don't want to. Or, if you'd rather, I'm sure I can help you come up with an…alternate plan," she said with a wink, her implication clear.

"I want to know what part you played in this. Obviously some manipulation went on, but what do you get out of it, Ms. McKinley?"

"Maybe I have my own agenda."

"Which would be?"

"That's for me to know and for you to find out. So, where to?" she asked Alex with a challenge in her voice.

Alex tapped three times on the partition, and when it lowered, he told the driver, "The W Atlanta, please."

Sue didn't comment, but wore a satisfied smile.

Also, don't miss my upcoming book,

"*Quarantine with the Billionaire*"

DIAMONDS NICOLE WATSON

Coming Soon!

Find out more by going to my website:

DIAMONDSNWATSON.COM

Diamonds is a new author in the Women's Fiction genre. She is a lover of all things romantic, and steamy.